SLIGHTLY LIKE STRANGERS

Focusing on novels with contemporary concerns, Bantam New Fiction introduces some of the most exciting voices at work today. Look for these titles wherever Bantam New Fiction is sold:

WHITE PALACE by Glenn Savan
SOMEWHERE OFF THE COAST OF MAINE by Ann Hood
COYOTE by Lynn Vannucci
VARIATIONS IN THE NIGHT by Emily Listfield
LIFE DURING WARTIME by Lucius Shepard
THE HALLOWEEN BALL by James Howard Kunstler
PARACHUTE by Richard Lees
THUNDER ISLAND by James Howard Kunstler
WAITING TO VANISH by Ann Hood
BLOCKBUSTER by Patricia Marx and Douglas G. McGrath
GOOD ROCKIN' TONIGHT by William Hauptman
SLIGHTLY LIKE STRANGERS by Emily Listfield

BANTAM NEW FICTION

SLIGHTLY LIKE STRANGERS

EMILY LISTFIELD

BANTAM BOOKS
TORONTO • NEW YORK • LONDON • SYDNEY • AUCKLAND

SLIGHTLY LIKE STRANGERS
A Bantam Book / November 1988

Library of Congress Cataloging-in-Publication Data

Listfield, Emily.
  Slightly like strangers.

  (Bantam new fiction)
  I. Title.
PS3562.I7822S55 1988   813'.54   88-14647
ISBN 0-553-34538-9

Published simultaneously in the United States and Canada

Bantam Books are published by Bantam Books, a division of Bantam
Doubleday Dell Publishing Group, Inc. Its trademark, consisting of the
words "Bantam Books" and the portrayal of a rooster, is Registered
in U.S. Patent and Trademark Office and in other countries. Marca
Registrada. Bantam Books, 666 Fifth Avenue, New York, New York 10103.

PRINTED IN THE UNITED STATES OF AMERICA

FG   0 9 8 7 6 5 4 3 2 1

PART ONE

Like a stranger's eyelash falling out of a library book and onto your pillow—unexpected, foreign, curiously intimate—that's what it was like having him here.

Amanda watched Sam crouching on the other side of the living room. His fine blond hair curled eccentrically behind his left ear and whenever he was distracted or anxious or just lost someplace he reached unconsciously to flatten it down. That's where his hand was now as he flipped the ragged tops of album covers quickly in succession. His navy polo shirt was coming out of the back of his jeans and a plate of his pale skin shone in the artificial light. The midsummer night was just beginning to cool and the windows were flung wide open to tempt the breeze in. Outside, a car alarm was going off and off and off, and Sam was muttering to himself.

"What are you looking for?" Amanda asked finally.

Sam continued knocking back groups of records. "A little peace and quiet," he said.

She turned the page of the magazine before her without looking down, without looking at him. "I thought that's what you moved to New York to escape."

Sam smiled and dismissed an aging group of 45's. "Where's that B. B. King record you were playing the other day?"

"I told you," Amanda said, "blues are in the corner."

Sam groaned and crouch-walked across the living room floor, flinching slightly when his knees cracked. He had been living here for almost two months now, gradually carving out space where he could, in the medicine cabinet, the bottom of the closet, in the half-hidden expectancy of her voice when she came home—are you there?—but he had yet to conquer the odd configurations of her records, her drawers, her books, a seemingly purposeful impenetrability. He began once more flipping aside albums, every now and then coming across one that had never even been opened.

"You know what I'm going to do tomorrow?" he asked.

"What?"

"Put these damn records in alphabetical order."

Amanda laughed. His need for systems, for graphs, for tangible explanations, was one of the things, like the way he bit his lip when he read or touched her foot with his in the morning if he wanted to make love, it was one of the things.

"You do that," she said, and pretended to return to the pale green pages of the magazine.

Sam eventually gave up his search and switched on the radio. The high vehement voices of a gospel choir crashed suddenly into the room and he turned the volume down before walking over to the table where Amanda was sitting. He put his hands lightly on her shoulders and rested his chin on her head.

"What are you reading, anyway?" he asked.

She turned the pages so that he could see the cover of *Backlog,* scattered with fuzzy snapshots of last month's parties.

"I don't know why you read that crap," Sam said.

Amanda smiled. "Someone I know and love happens to write this crap."

He laughed slightly and kissed the top of her head before straightening up. They still used the word like lace, like an occasional gift, a token to be taken lightly, of course, laughed at as if to lessen the heft of giving, of receiving, of possessing. It was a pause to them, this

4

word, love, and their eyes met for an instant, shining, parrying, before pulling back into calmer air.

"Don't remind me," Sam said.

He began to wander aimlessly about the room, his hands, his eyes, grazing this and that, a mottled paperback, a pair of sunglasses, an unframed picture curling at the corners—his, hers, so heedlessly overlapping. It was these evenings, in, home, alone, these most ordinary of evenings, that were the clumsiest to them both.

When he could find nothing to distract himself with, he went inside to the small bedroom and kicked off his sneakers before lying down and picking up the book that he had left straddled across the lacquered night table. Across the open page he found the red skid marks of Amanda's nail polish. He smiled to himself at the evidence she left behind, indentations of affection, secretive, shy of light. They were both still scavenging for sign posts, for clues.

He didn't say anything later, when she came to bed, when she fitted her body inch by inch to his and kissed him tentatively on the cheek, not too hungry, not too brisk, he didn't say anything as he flicked off the overhead light and let his arm fall across her waist. There was no rush, no rush at all. He only smiled up into the darkness when she reached over and straightened out his curl.

While Sam slept, Amanda lay awake and imagined her limbs falling off. Just like that. Her arms, her legs, simply snapping off. Lying about like the unused portions of a mannequin in a store window. She sat up slowly and began to shake her arms up and down in the air, moving her feet in tiny arcs beneath the sheets. It had been like this last night, and the night before too—this numbness, this cold that inched up from her tips. She squeezed the flesh of her forearms and tried to rotate the muscles in silence.

Sam opened his eyes to slits and watched for a moment, watched this strange predawn dance of hers.

"Are you okay?" he mumbled sleepily.

"Yeah. My arms are just a little numb. Maybe it's from quitting smoking. Go back to sleep."

He lay motionless as the dark looming shadows of her arms crossed and recrossed his face. "I didn't ask you to quit," he said.

"I know. I just thought, well you know, with you staying here and all." She sat still for a moment.

Sam tucked the pillow tighter beneath his head and closed his eyes. Staying here. The sheets were warm against his cheek.

And when Amanda was sure that he had fallen back to sleep, she once again resumed her shaking—slower, quieter—until she finally slipped into a fretful approximation of sleep herself.

The next morning, she woke to the hollow clicks of

Sam double-locking the front door on his way out. It was still disconsonant, his shirts hanging neatly in the closet, the computations and compulsive figurings he left adrift on scraps of paper, the carefully rolled cereal top; at thirty, it was all new to her, these scars of possession that she had always so vehemently slid away from, and like a spy she meticulously noted every movement, every step.

Amanda went into the kitchen to get the coffee that Sam had left warming for her and took a cup back to bed with a stack of fashion magazines and a notebook. She drank half a cup in the dark and then she switched on the lights and began to study the pages of *Vogue* with a slow, deliberate intensity. She turned the pages down when something interested her—the way these pants were cropped just above the ankle, the blazer snug about the waist—and made notes in a large and rambling script. This too was new for her, this patience, this attention, for she had been a partner in Legacies only for a few months and the sense of responsibility was still a foreign currency—she had barely held a steady job before. She crammed her notes into an alligator case emblazoned with the store's logo, and stood up on the bed to stretch. Her arms, her legs, were warm and sensate now.

It was just before noon when Amanda knocked loudly on the thick steel door of Nancy and Jack's loft. Inside, she could hear the baby bawling and Nancy walking rapidly back and forth, the leather soles of her sandals flapping against the uneven wooden floors. She knocked once more, taking off the top layer of skin on her knuckles.

Nancy finally opened the door. "Sorry," she said. "Ben doesn't seem to want to sleep today." When she kissed her friend hello, Amanda got a whiff of the sickeningly sweet traces of Enfamil in her hair. "The joys of motherhood," Nancy said, and deposited the baby in a bright yellow plastic swing contraption. "Do you want some iced coffee?"

"Sure. You don't have a cigarette, do you?"

"I thought you quit."

"I did."

"Oh. Well would you settle for a pacifier?"

"I've settled for worse."

Nancy looked over at Ben every couple of seconds while they talked, her eyes going up and down with his swinging. "I think he has a heat rash on his thighs," she said distractedly as she stared at the faint pink traces dotting his mounds of alabaster flesh. She tried to wipe some dried up dribble from her blouse before turning her attention to Amanda. "So," she asked, "what's with you?"

"Nothing much. The usual. Sam wants to play house, I want to play hooky, on good days we meet somewhere in between."

"And on bad days?"

Amanda smiled. "There are no bad days."

Nancy raised her eyebrows. "Talk about your metamorphosis."

"Okay. I love having him here, I really do. It's just kind of hard to get used to living with someone."

"Is he staying for good this time?" Nancy asked.

"What is this, the Spanish Inquisition? How should I know?" Amanda ripped up the stained paper napkin before her, rolling it between her fingers into tight wet little balls. "He says he is."

"For better or worse?"

Amanda rolled her eyes. "One thing at a time. We're still trying to conquer grocery shopping. We're not really planning that far ahead."

Nancy smiled. "Of course not. God forbid. But just remember," she added more seriously, "that's what got you two in trouble the last time."

Amanda bit her lip, tasting the perfumed wax of her lipstick. The last time. It had been a bloodless courtship of reticence and restraint and she had almost lost him in the overwhelming silence that had grown like thickened skin between them. She had almost lost him and she looked

8

back on their separation and reunion now with a retro-active terror that left her shy and unsteady in its wake. She shook her head.

"I know," Amanda said. "But it's different now. We really do talk more."

Nancy looked at her. "Sign language doesn't count."

"He's not exactly the spill-your-guts type either, you know." And then, blinking away the conversation, she reached down and got the case full of clippings from her large patent leather bag. "I wanted to show you some ideas for the store," she said to Nancy, her partner now, her boss.

And she spread the glossy pages and barely legible notes across the cluttered table, pointing to hems and bodices, while Nancy glanced down and then away, gri-macing, smiling, miming to the baby in the swing.

The soot, as if finally defeated by the summer, lay prostrate in gobs on the pavement, not even bothering to fly into pedestrians' eyes. Sam frowned unconsciously as he stepped over a particularly nasty pile—there were some things that he would never get used to. Nevertheless, he enjoyed walking the nineteen blocks to work each morning, taking the city in bits and pieces, in corners at a time. For he no longer expected it to come to him whole, luminous, he no longer thought he could shake and shake it until all of its goodies tumbled out of the skyscrapers' windows and into his pockets. It wasn't that he had lost the will, or the strength. What he saw now was that he had never really had it—perhaps he had come too late, or left too soon—whatever; when he looked up now he could count the things that would never be his. And strangely, this did not make him sad, or bitter, but brought instead a certain sense of relief, an ease of breath.

It had been different when Sam had first moved to New York two years ago. For although he had procrastinated leaving home, Allensville, Ohio, until he was twenty-eight, the city was still a dotted neon promise to him, it was all that was heady and intricate and seductive. It was also the last route away from the safe house closing brick by brick around him, away from the small-town paper he was steadily rising at, and away from Cathy, who he was supposed to love but did not want. It was someplace to go.

But Sam had become rapidly chiseled away by the

city's resolute indifference to his presence, by the inanity of his work for *Backlog,* by too many returned résumés, and by his mysterious courtship with Amanda. She had grown up in the city and took its reproaches for granted, she did not try to hold onto him, not hard enough, not tight enough—she did not ask him to stay. For Sam had secretly wanted to grid the city into a safer, more intelligible map, to lessen the very uncertainties, the very risks, that had beckoned him. And when he had found that the rules and the guidelines he had come armed with curved between his fingers he had left, gone back—only to find that the city, its percussions, its prejudices, Amanda, had become his. This time, though, he would take it in chips, in fragments; he would not expect it to come to him whole and pliant.

Sam nodded to the uniformed guard in the lobby and took the crowded elevator up to the eleventh floor. Since *Backlog* had gone national, they had moved to a large gray building midtown where most of the other offices were filled with ladies' sportswear and lower-priced lingerie. *Backlog* had filled its half of a floor with kidney-shaped desks and leopard skin rugs, autographed photographs of music and fashion stars, movie stills from biker sagas, waxed red flowers and a scantily clad NYU intern for a receptionist who looked up from her gallery guide and said good morning to Sam.

He spread his work out on the shiny black laminated surface of his desk and stared down at the thin pile of articles before him. The top piece was entitled, "How hair color affects sexual performance: The experts speak out." Sam smiled. It was far away from the petty crimes and municipal scandals he used to write about, far away from the big city politics he had once dreamed of writing about. But it was a steady job after all, The Metropolitan Editor, it was something. He would take the city in bits and pieces, in corners at a time. He sharpened his pencil and began to edit the musings of the wig manufacturers and radio sexologists and celebrities he had never heard of.

Before going to lunch Sam walked slowly past the managing editor's office while pretending to refill his coffee cup, his eyes sliding past the glass walls to this rumpled, attractive man, Patrick, his feet on the desk, the phone balanced on his shoulder, amiably throwing darts at a picture of Marlene Dietrich, and then he left the office alone. As much as possible, Sam slithered away from invitations to join his co-workers, preferring to wander by himself through the crevices of different neighborhoods, or sit in the corner of a restaurant and listen to other people's conversations. Today, he bought a hot dog and walked over to the jammed-up steps of the public library. He found a little rectangle in the sun and settled in, happiest to lose himself amid the jugglers, the boom boxes, the secretaries with their yogurts and the pushers with their pills, happiest to pull the city's proffered quilt of anonymity over his head and peer out through the holes his curiosity bore, safely out of reach if only for a little while. At exactly two o'clock, he stood up, threw away his trash, and went back.

On his way home that night, Sam stopped by the Korean market and picked up some long-stemmed yellow tiger lilies for Amanda and a couple of imported beers for himself. Inside, he could hear her in the kitchen and he locked the door behind him before going in and handing her the flowers. It was the way she smiled, like a young girl getting her first bouquet, it was the way the smallest pat of attention could still take her by surprise, heat her skin, it was the way her own pleasure embarrassed her and she went quickly by him to get a vase.

"So how did it go today?" she asked when she returned from the living room. "Did you get a chance to talk to Patrick about that piece you wanted to do?"

Sam was rattling around in the silverware, looking for a bottle opener. "He was busy all day," he answered in the flattened, easy voice he saved for dismissals. He opened his beer and took a long sip before sidling up behind Amanda. He kissed her on the back of her neck and she arched to him like a cat. "I do love you, you know," he said.

He was sitting up with his back to her, pulling himself steadily away from sleep, his tousled head resting heavily in his hands—he was hers to watch for a moment. Amanda propped herself up on her elbow, and then, pulling the navy sheets with her, she leaned over and traced the sloping hard curve of his upper arm with her fingertips. The room was filled with the deep khaki light of a sunless morning and children were already playing noisily beneath their window.

"That's my favorite spot," she said as she came to rest in the valley just below his neck. His body was compact and firm and solid; nothing had ever felt that real to her.

Sam turned his head around to her. The lines that cut straight down his cheeks were deepened by a lazy smile. "Your very favorite?" he asked.

She smiled too. "Well almost."

There was still the thin white film of night over Amanda's eyes and her pale brown hair fell in feathers about her narrow face. Sam reached over and gently traced her full lips with his forefinger. He remembered how long it had taken before she could move toward him first, show the compliment of desire, and it made it all the sweeter now. He moved his hand down her long torso and gave her calf—it was what he could find—a squeeze. She was so much softer in the morning, almost comically blurry, the edges not yet picked up and sharpened.

"What do you want to do today?" he asked.

14

"I don't know." Amanda lay back and folded her arms beneath her head so that he was faced with a long stretch of bare skin, sheer white and vulnerable. "Whatever you want to do."

The expectation that they would, of course, spend a free day together was shiny as a new toy to them, and if neither was particularly in the mood to play with it that day, they would not admit it, not yet. Besides, they did want to, for it was still shiny and new and all of its quirks had yet to be discovered.

"What time is it, anyway?" Amanda asked.

"About nine."

"Nine o'clock on a Sunday morning? We should go back to sleep."

Sam laughed. "I think I'll go get the *Times*." He was ready for movement, for the news, he was ready to get started, always, while she would hide a little longer.

Amanda murmured something unintelligible and pulled the sheets completely over her head. Sam looked down for a minute at the lumpy blue outline of her face and kissed what he hoped was her nose before getting up to take a shower.

In the afternoon, when they were finally at the same level of alertness, they took a bus uptown to the Metropolitan Museum. Inside, the large entrance hall was filled with other couples and parents with babies on their backs, sated tourists, earnest students with sketchbooks tucked beneath their arms, and girlfriends killing the Sunday afternoon in pairs, waiting for the night, for tomorrow. It had always slipped Amanda into the blues before, the wide eyes and the cold gray stone and the perfectly groomed flowers, all stitched up in loneliness. But now, when she took Sam's hand, she found in it some of the comfort and arrogance of belonging as they went upstairs to wander through the portraits of another time.

"She looks so repressed," Sam commented as they

stood before a pale woman with piled-up ebony hair and narrow lips.

Amanda let go of his hand and headed for the next painting. "I wish people were more repressed now," she said. "Life would be so much more pleasant."

Sam laughed, but not completely—he knew that she probably meant it. For despite the fact that it was good between them now, better than it had ever been, he had long suspected that she saw each act of tenderness, of kindness, as an act of surrender, and he suspected too that she catalogued each and every one. He walked into the next gallery and went up to the glass case centered on the floor, pulled down into the absolute symmetry of an architectural sketch.

"Marvelous, no?" The elderly gentleman turned his crinkled eyes to Sam. "Just marvelous." He was wearing a loose seersucker suit with a white linen shirt and there were bits of Europe stuck between his syllables. "I used to do work like that myself."

"Were you an architect?"

"I was. Quite a while ago, I'm afraid."

"Not so long ago, I'm sure." Sam smiled, and it was genuine and kind, but it cost him nothing, for he had a large stack of them in reserve, a factory of smiles ever ready to charm and encourage strangers, especially strangers—it was one of his talents. "What kind of buildings did you design?"

"Many things, many things. But summer homes, resorts, were my forté." And he began to describe the settings and solutions, the highlights of his career.

Amanda, who had finished with her wall of women, walked into the next gallery and spotted Sam, chatting effortlessly to an old man with thinning gray hair and a worn fedora in his hands. She smiled at the sight, at Sam, who always took such delight in chatting up newcomers, who listened, not as she did, to get to the point and move on, but with a certain pleasure she had never tasted. It was one of the things that moved her, this openness and enthusiasm, this purity, it was one of the things she would learn, for she had an innate suspicion of strangers that often came across as sullenness. She walked over and slipped her arm, pleased and proprietary, through his.

Mr. Franchessi tipped his head and smiled. "How do you do?"

"Mr. Franchessi was just telling me about a house he built on the coast of Portugal," Sam said eagerly. "It rested on stilts he had painted in all different pastels, isn't that right? And a deck overlooking the ocean."

"Oh? I love the Algarve," Amanda said. "What town was it in? Maybe I know it."

"Albufeira. Have you been? It was once the loveliest little fishing village, though of course now . . ."

"Yes. I was there years ago. When I was a teenager."

"You were?" Sam asked. He had never been to Europe.

Amanda smiled and nodded. "Tell me," she said as the three of them began to tour the rest of the exhibit together, "the lights, all the electricity, used to fade on and off in the evening, as if they were too tired to support the weight . . ."

"The weight of all those tourists," Mr. Franchessi laughed. "Yes, it happened when I was there too. I quite liked it, all the officials running around in circles, courting the new buildings, and those lights that trembled in rebellion."

"That's just what they did," Amanda agreed. "There was a café, I can't remember the name of it, off on a tiny side street, where . . ."

Sam watched, watched Amanda begin to dance so lightly through a world he had never known, and as she felt him watching, a diaphanous charm grew beneath his gaze, and it shone with a luster she could never have found alone. She touched Mr. Franchessi's sleeve. "What a terrific life," she said. "To go from one beautiful spot to another, building little fantasies as you go. I can't think of anything more romantic."

17

"If I'd had you by my side, it would have been."

"I'm sure you had ladies throwing themselves off of the cliffs each time you left."

"But one never really does leave, does one?"

"No?"

"Of course not. You're young still, you'll see."

"I'm old enough to have seen people leave."

"Ah," Mr. Franchessi smiled. "Wait, my dear. Be patient. You'll see. They always come back. One way or another, it's impossible to truly leave anything behind." They had reached the end of the exhibit and they stood in the room of postcards and posters and scarves, unsure of how to separate. Mr. Franchessi raised Amanda's hand to his weathered lips and kissed it. "You're a lucky man," he said as he shook Sam's hand.

"Yes, I know."

Sam and Amanda walked home through midtown streets that were empty now, the glass buildings barren and opaque. It was one of those days that had never quite managed to arrive and the night settled easily down to claim its place. Normally, Amanda walked faster than Sam. Hers, after all, was a different city than his, and she did not have to look up as often—she knew what was there, what had always been there. Tonight, though, she slowed her pace to his, glad for the firmness of his hand in hers, glad to be going home together. It was good between them now, better than it had ever been.

"Do you remember that weekend we spent together in East Hampton last winter?" she asked.

"Sure." He gave her hand a squeeze and laughed. "I remember that you were embarrassed to waltz with me, even though we were alone in the room."

Amanda laughed too. "I did though," she said, looking up at him.

Sam looked down and smiled. For all her easy talk about European resorts and her steady stride through traffic, for all of the city's high-gloss shellac, he knew how

18

hard it had been for her to take his hand and follow, and each tentative step was a magnifying glass on his heart. "You did," he said, and he kissed her as they waited for the light to change.

That night, after they made love, he lay still, inside of her, for a while. And when he pulled out of her, away, there was all the emptiness, all the sadness in the world, and she could not help but sigh. "Did I hurt you?" he asked, concerned. "No," she said quietly, "no."

There was still the problem of Cathy. Sam had always prided himself on doing his duty, on doing what was expected, it was what he had always done. Only once, when he had left abruptly for New York, had he deviated, and the mess of running away was still sticky around his mouth. He sat on the worn rug of the bedroom floor, the radio tuned in to a call-in homeowners' show, the door closed. When he had first called Cathy six weeks ago to tell her that he was not coming back after all, he had used words like *Allensville* and *New York,* but they both knew it was not a simple matter of geography. "I'll write," he had promised her, "and try to explain. I can't right now." He turned off the radio. At the other end of the apartment he could hear Amanda open and shut the refrigerator door, singing an old Bob Dylan song off-key. He smiled and brushed off the clean piece of stationery that was balanced atop the dictionary on his knees.

"Dear Cathy," he began in a small, neat hand, "I know that I promised you more of an explanation than I was able to give you when I left. I'm not sure if it's one that you will understand or accept, but here goes. Part of the problem for me in Allensville was that the future suddenly seemed so clear, so evident. There was nothing inherently wrong with it, it was just too predictable. The most I could aspire to was somewhere down the road becoming the managing editor of the *Weekly Ledger.* I'm sure that's a fine thing to do, but it's not what I want. At least not now. Cathy, you deserve someone who knows what they want. You want a kind of life that I cannot in good conscience say I can give you. I don't know how to explain it except to say that I was beginning to feel more and more like an impostor, nodding in agreement because I didn't want to hurt you, daily becoming further away from anything that made sense to me, until it seemed that nothing made any sense at all. It appears I have hurt you anyway and I'm truly sorry for that. It was a mistake for us to try again that last time, however briefly. I should have spoken up at an earlier date. You have always been sweet and kind and I didn't mean to in any way mislead you. I don't know what it is I'll find in New York. I don't even know what exactly it is I want, but maybe that's the point. What I do know is that I have to give it a try, a real try, this time. It might be the last chance I get. I'm sorry for any pain I might have caused you. Yours, Sam."

He stretched his legs out before him and rested his head on the corner of the mattress as he reread the letter. Long ago, Sam had devised a way to drape his obligations in such stilted tones, such icy ellipses and faultless manners, that they seemed to have nothing to do with him, he had found a way to stay safely hidden behind the conventions, and if at times it made him queasy, it was still where he preferred to be. Nevertheless, a brief tremor of guilt compelled him to add, "P.S. Say hi to your parents and brother for me," before he sealed the letter and wrote the address automatically across the dark gray envelope.

There were other letters, bank statements, bills. Sam crawled over to the closet and dug his calculator out of the cardboard box in the back and returned to his pile. As he added, subtracted, regretted certain purchases, he placed each carefully written check in a mounting pile on the floor and then went back to his columns, trying to find in them something that was his, a buffer, but the city seemed to snap at his little store of security with brattish mocking jaws. Disgusted, he stood up and turned the radio back on, accidentally scattering the pile with his foot.

A desk. A little corner that was his, a reason to unpack. He left the montage of envelopes behind and rifled once more through the box in the closet until he came across the old blue plastic ruler that he'd had since high school. He began to measure the far wall, pushing aside the low dresser that Amanda's clothes and perfume bottles and magazines were slashed across. Just something simple, something that was his, a corner of his own. He wrote down the measurings on a scrap of paper and stuck them in his back pocket.

Amanda had long since stopped singing and he could hear her banging the pots and pans about like a frustrated five-year-old stuck inside on a rainy day. He smiled. A little corner of his own, he would steal it if he had to, from the clutter and the elusiveness, he would build himself a desk, a reason to unpack. He lay down on the bed and listened to the radio.

When a commercial came on, Sam got up and gathered his envelopes, carefully sticking the letter to Cathy in the middle of the pile—though there was really no need for subterfuge, it always came so naturally to them. For he knew that Amanda wouldn't ask about it, then, ever. But if he had once thought that this reticence was proof that she did not care, he realized now that it was something else, something altogether different. He brushed his hair back with his hands and straightened his shirt and then he went to find her.

Amanda stood in the kitchen deveining three pounds of shrimp. She had never deveined shrimp before and the amount of steel gray cartilage astounded her. All about was a novice's confusion—unnecessary pots and pans and sacks of extra ingredients and the three cookbooks she had bought last week propped open with soggy sponges. In the four years she had been living in this apartment, she had never had her sister and brother-in-law over for dinner. In fact, she had worn her lack of domesticity like a badge, shifting it this way and that so that its light hit Sally in the eyes whenever possible. For if Amanda had disdained the kitchen as a matter of principle, Sally had run to it early, furiously, shimmying up the first available lines seeking a sanctuary, seeking to reconstruct a home from whatever seemed likely—for neither of them was ever quite certain what a home was supposed to be.

"Goddam shrimp," Amanda muttered.

Sam heard her as he passed by. "What?"

"Never mind."

He wanted to go up and put his arms around her and make her laugh at the chaos on the counters, but he knew that he must take this effort seriously, knew that he must not tease her, so earnest and so flustered.

"I'm going out to mail some letters," he said. "Do you need anything?"

"Tranquilizers."

Sam laughed. "Relax. It's only Sally and Frank. I don't see what you're so nervous about."

"Forget it. Pick up a couple of bottles of wine, okay? Maybe we can get him drunk."

"Fat chance."

Amanda waited half a minute after hearing the front door close before pulling out a fresh pack of Marlboros she had stashed behind some wilted spinach in the back of the refrigerator. She pushed the window open even wider and leaned out on the ledge as she lit the chilled tobacco and waved the smoke outside. When she had smoked it almost down to the filter, she ran it under the faucet and then hid the butt beneath a pile of garbage that lay splashed about the floor. She never should have invited them to begin with, she didn't know why she had.

That evening, the four of them sat self-consciously before their mismatched plates. Sally was like a softer, hazier version of her older sister. Where Amanda could appear angular, aloof, removed, Sally was round and tactile and mobile. The hair that was straight and light brown on Amanda became blonder, curlier, on her sister. And yet there was something—a certain watchfulness, a certain detachment—beneath Amanda's composure, beneath Sally's fluttering femininity, something that was mirrored deep within. It was as if they had started out long ago at the same point and careened in wildly opposite directions, both intent foremost on escape. Only lately were the two able to glance back over their shoulders and realize that perhaps they were not so distant after all, only lately could they begin to acknowledge that mirrored point, now so dusty and distorted.

"It's delicious," Sally said cheerfully, anxious always to smooth, to please.

Amanda laughed. "You haven't even tasted it yet."

All four of them turned their attention down to their plates, ready to admire, and the only sounds for a moment were knives, steak knives, trying desperately to slice into the shrimp.

"Jesus," Amanda said, the first to give up.

"It's fine, really," Sally said as she tried to chew another bite.

Amanda glanced across the table at Frank, certain that she would find a satisfied smirk carved into his face. For they had always viewed each other with dislike and suspicion, Frank, so staunch in his beliefs of right and wrong, proper and improper, and Amanda, holding all the ambiguities he would conquer in his wife.

"It said broil for ten minutes on each side," she said.

"That's absurd," Frank answered as he unconsciously straightened the collar of his green Lacoste shirt. He had lately taken up gourmet cooking on weekends and had designed a course of study for himself that was thorough, absolute, and joyless. "No one broils shrimp for ten minutes on each side," he assured her.

Amanda rose from the table and got the cookbook, stuck open with grease to the page. "See," she said, "ten minutes."

"Well, it must have been a typo. You should write them a letter."

Amanda closed the book and dropped it at his feet. "Why don't you do it for me, Frank? It sounds like just your kind of thing." She thrust her hands into the pockets of her checkered pedal pushers and glared at him.

Sally took a huge gulp of wine to keep herself from laughing and Sam stood up and began to clear the plates. "What the hell," he said, a smile on his face as easy as silk, "I was really in the mood for Chinese food anyway." Amanda laughed gratefully as he got the take-out menu from the refrigerator door and called to order an extravagant amount of food and beer, patiently giving the address three times, despite the fact that he was sure they knew it by now.

"So," he said, hanging up the phone, "did you bring

any new pictures of Maggie? It must be six months since I've seen her."

A couple of hours later, when Frank had finally convinced Sally that it really was time to go—please dear, you've had enough to drink—Amanda and Sam took their tea and their fortune cookies to bed and sat with their knees up, the cups balanced precariously between them.

"He's like a Mormon without religion," Sam said. "I don't know how she stands it."

Amanda touched his knee with hers—he feels like I do—and smiled. "Thanks," she said.

"For what?"

"I don't know, being such a good diplomat I guess. I probably would have cracked a bottle over his head if you weren't there."

"As long as it's the proper vintage."

Amanda laughed. "I thought Sally had finally had enough last year, but then she changed her mind. He convinced her it would mean twenty years of therapy for Maggie."

"What did she ever see in him to begin with?"

"I don't know. She was only twenty-one when she married him. He was probably the first man she ever slept with. Even when we were kids, she had this fantasy of a perfect little bourgeois TV kind of marriage." Amanda picked a piece of lint from her knee. "I guess because it was so different from home."

Sam took a sip of his tea, pale and weak. "It doesn't have to be that way, you know," he said.

She brushed her hair away from her eyes. "I know. Anyway, she got what she thought she wanted, and now she thinks she's stuck with it."

"And what do you want?"

She looked at him and smiled. "A fortune cookie," she said, reaching for the nearest one.

Sam watched as she opened it. "What does it say?" he asked, flicking aside the crumbs.

"Everything you touch will turn to gold."

"They obviously didn't try your shrimp," Sam said, and Amanda laughed—it was okay, it was fine—for she'd had many lovers before, too many, but never one who was a friend like Sam.

"Well in that case, see if I touch anything else tonight," she said, and Sam laughed too.

There was a long corridor
of them, years of them,
these rooms of Bill's that were always warm and melan-
choly and would have been so soothing if they didn't
have sex lurking beneath the piles and the darkness.
Amanda remembered long ago when he had still been
painting, the small studio with its tubes of ochers and
blues and magical wooden boxes stuffed with broken
charcoals and inks. Another room, with Japanese lanterns
and a mattress on the floor, they were younger then,
pennies for throwing the *I Ching*, unused musical instru-
ments and esoteric records in a variety of languages.
Rooms that you could climb into and never want to leave
except that you knew you really shouldn't be there to
begin with . . .

He was just undoing his top button when the doorbell rang. "Who is it?" he yelled impatiently across the
living room.

"Amanda."

Bill came to the door with his paisley tie askew, his
hair that was the exact color as hers quickly patted down
almost into place.

"Amanda?" He undid three locks and let her in. "My
God, it's been a long time."

She smiled and kissed him hello as his hand drifted
down her back.

"I brought us a present," she said. "Get out your
wine glasses. As I remember, they're usually under your
bed, right next to the oriental erotica."

Bill smiled. "I've graduated to Indian. I'll show it to you later." He went into the black and white tiled kitchen and returned with two thick cobalt blue goblets.

Amanda pulled a couple of bottles of Pomeral from her bag.

"What are we drinking to?" he asked as he poured them both full glasses.

"I don't know. How about true love and other vices?"

"I'd rather drink to true vice and other loves."

"Whatever."

They both took long sips and relaxed into the cracking leather couch, their feet atop the dusty books and crumpled shirts and filled ashtrays crammed onto the chipped walnut coffee table. Stripes of light squeezed through the vertical blinds and the wine was rich and soothing. There was no need for music, for preliminary bantering, for reasons or excuses. They were used to each other, to afternoons like this, or evenings, theirs had been a long rotation of pleasure unfettered by need—easy, enjoyable, known.

Bill slipped his loosely knotted tie over his head and dropped it over Amanda's. "I've missed you," he said.

She smiled briefly and then switched outside. "So. How's your job going? What brilliant designs have you come up with lately?"

Bill laughed at the abrupt change, it was so much like her, so much like him. "I was just doing some sketches for a new album cover this afternoon." He leaned over and knocked a couple of books onto the floor until he found the one he was looking for. "I'm using a quote from Dante." He opened to an earmarked page and began to read in a voice that had temporarily lost its confident, ironic padding, a voice that she had heard only rarely on late sad nights. "These wretched ones, who never were alive, went naked and were stung again, again by horse-flies and by wasps that circled them."

"Who never were alive?"

29

"Cowards." He put the book down and shrugged. "It's for a heavy metal band," he said as he turned to her, smiling. "They said it was cool with them." He refilled their glasses and lay back with his hand on her thigh, bared by a short skirt. It lay there, heavy and still, as the room grew dark with the coming nightfall.

"Your turn," he said. "How are things going with Legacies?"

"Okay. Good, actually."

"You sound surprised."

"I'm always surprised when things go well. But I do have the feeling that Nancy's not crazy about the assistant I hired."

"What's wrong with her?"

"Nothing's wrong with her. She's just a little inexperienced."

"So why did you choose her?"

"I don't know. She had a funny plastic bag, she made me laugh, who knows why anyone chooses anyone? She'll work out."

He squeezed her leg. "Sure." He uncorked the second bottle of wine. "Anyway, work was never what we did best."

Conversation ebbed gradually away from them, sliding down into a familiar, comfortable silence. He leaned over and slowly touched his lips to hers, soft and red and acidic, and she found a piece of herself that she had left behind in his mouth a million times before and she rolled it on her tongue and tasted it and pulled away, moaning slightly with the uncertainty of temptation rising from her belly. "I can't," she said.

Bill ran his tongue over his lips where she had just been and then sat back. "Sam?"

Amanda shrugged.

"Why did you come today?"

"I don't know. I guess to find out."

Bill nodded and handed her a full glass. "You know,"

he said, "you and I have always been a lot alike. You're not the settling down type."

"People change," she said defiantly. "I can change. I love him." She took a sip of her wine and relaxed.

"Why him? If you don't mind my asking."

"Maybe because we're so different. He makes me feel grounded."

"I always thought being grounded was the one thing you were most afraid of."

Amanda smiled. "Okay, not grounded. I don't know how to explain it to you. He makes me feel that things I never thought were possible, at least not for me, are possible."

"Like what?"

"I don't know. Just normal things. A normal life."

Bill laughed. "Since when did you want a normal life? I thought that's what you were running away from all this time."

"Maybe I'm tired of running. Maybe that's just not how I want to live anymore. I don't know. All I know is that I'm better when I'm with him. His world just seems less murky. Cleaner. You know?"

Bill smiled. "I like the badder you."

"Exactly."

"Well, I suppose anything can happen."

Amanda shrugged. "I suppose anything can."

He squeezed her knee and it only shot through her a little bit.

Later, when half of the second bottle was gone and the details of the room had vanished into the night, he walked her to the door, both of them wobbly on their feet.

"You know," he said as he traced her collarbone with his thumb, "I do hope it works out for you."

"Sure you do."

"No, I mean it. It'll be like some high-grade experiment. You can be our pilot fish into the world of normalcy."

"I wouldn't go that far." She smiled and kissed him before pressing for the elevator.

"But on the other hand, if you should change your mind . . ."

Amanda was laughing as the door slid closed between them.

It wasn't much of a crash, but when Sam went into the bathroom to see what had happened, Amanda was clutching at her hair with both hands.

"Are you okay?" he asked.

She let out her breath and turned to him. "I just dropped the aspirin bottle," she said crisply. She lowered her arms but made no move to pick up the scattered pills.

"It's not that big a deal," he said.

Amanda reddened and walked out of the bathroom, leaving Sam to collect the aspirin, already disintegrating into soggy white chalk on the damp floor.

When he had first met Amanda, first watched her, it was her composure, her self-containment and confidence, that had intrigued him. Cool, guarded, dry, it was as smooth and tempting to him as a freshly ironed sheet, waiting to be touched, it was a distance he thought he could traverse. But lying across it was a smile, fleeting, enigmatic, a half-smile that seemed to mock all the conclusions he had thought were inevitable, until for the first time nothing was inevitable, nothing at all. He had longed to trace that smile with his fingertips until he learned the secret of its disregard, he still did—but it was gone before he could touch it. Now he was beginning to see too how she hid from any bright lights, squirmed when he looked at her too long, too closely, shied from any raised voice, and panicked when anything, a bottle, a box, slipped suddenly from her grasp. He bent down and shoveled as many aspirin as he could back into the bottle and flushed the rest down the toilet.

When Sam went out into the living room, Amanda was sitting at the table, calmly sipping a diet cola and filing her nails. He knew by now that questions too direct would only waken sarcasm; instead he sniffed, circled— looking for a crack he could slip inside of.

"What time are we supposed to be there anyway?" he asked.

"I don't know." She held up a forefinger and inspected it. "Seven, I guess."

"Don't you think you should get dressed?"

"I will."

Sam watched her for another moment before deciding to leave her alone. Sometimes, it was like a thin sheet of ice—the images swirling just beneath, out of reach— and he had run from it, bruised, once before. He went into the bedroom to pick out a tie.

They were still shadows to him, this family of hers, still sketches waiting for flesh, for she had avoided any introductions or explanations, any intimations of embarrassment or pain. He had only a handful of facts, tasteless, odorless. Mr. Easton, an alcoholic whose drinking had erupted in unpredictable torrents throughout Amanda's childhood. Mrs. Easton, loyal, silent, shaken. He knew that they had divorced two years ago, that Mr. Easton had disappeared—it happens, doesn't it?—only to resurface married to another woman. And now? Somehow he was back, back home—and Mrs. Easton had held the door open, welcoming his return.

Sam returned to the living room. "Should I not drink in front of him?" he asked as he reknotted his tie for the third time.

"It doesn't matter," Amanda answered sharply. But the edge was more than she had intended and she pulled it back to soften it. "I mean, I realized a long time ago that it really doesn't matter what you do, good or bad.

34

Whatever sets him off is something only he can see or hear. It doesn't make a damn bit of difference what you do. Sally and my mother would have been a whole lot better off if they had realized that all along." Nevertheless, Amanda had become cautious, distrustful of any illusory peace. "I know this is your big night," she said as she finally got up to get dressed. "But don't get your hopes up. Chances are always good that he woke up in another state."

"Oh c'mon. It's not that bad. Is it?"

Amanda smiled. "No. Of course not. Besides, when he's good, he's very, very good. He'll probably have you pledging undying love to him before the night is out."

They were silent for most of the cab ride uptown. Amanda leaned back against the torn vinyl seat and removed her black velvet head band, put it back on, removed it. Finally, Sam put his hand over hers and she smiled. "I haven't seen him since he came back," she said quietly. "Christ, I don't even know which wife he's married to."

Sam's fingers contracted involuntarily. "Are you serious? Why didn't you ask your mother?"

Amanda shrugged. "It's on the list of things one doesn't discuss with her." She fixed her head band one last time. "And in the best of families too," she said, turning a hard shiny look to him.

Sam went expecting glass people, fragile and scratched.

When Mr. Easton answered the door, Sam found a jovial man with spots on his forehead like a smattering of light brown fingerprints and the worn-out remnants of attractiveness glistening in his eyes.

"Sweetheart," he said, taking Amanda in his arms excitedly and kissing her hello. "It's so good to see you." His voice was at once roguish and sincere and Amanda kissed him back with just slightly less enthusiasm.

"Hello, Dad. This is Sam Chapman."

"Come in, Sam," Mr. Easton said, his long arm reaching around Sam's shoulder. "Come in."

Sam and Amanda sat a few feet apart amid the faded blue flowers of an old chintz sofa. Though all of the lamps were turned on, the room was dim, as if a layer of dust had settled over everything—the portraits on the walls, the china in the cupboards, the Eastons—catching, suspending it all in a finely powdered gray. It was like the room of a loved one who had died—try as they might, no one had the heart to change a thing, no one ever would—and Mr. Easton's initial enthusiasm seemed to sink beneath its weight.

"Some sherry, dear?" Mrs. Easton asked no one in particular. She was a tall, thin woman with hazel eyes soft and worn as if scrubbed in bleach. Her short gray hair was simply, though meticulously, arranged, and she wore a lemon summer suit. Sam noticed that her legs were still quite shapely.

"Thank you, Mrs. Easton, I'd love some," Sam said.

It was a voice that Amanda recognized, sanded by politesse, well-mannered and easy. Too easy. She kept her eyes away from him.

"None for me," Mr. Easton said loudly. "I'll just get myself some club soda."

When they had returned with the drinks, Mr. and Mrs. Easton sat down simultaneously in overstuffed armchairs. They did not seem to look at each other, to acknowledge each other; they moved about like solitary apparitions, mindful, polite, absent. And yet, Mrs. Easton seemed to edge slightly toward her husband when he shifted position, tilt her head in his direction when he spoke—like a new mother listening always for a break in her baby's breathing.

Mr. Easton smiled over at his favorite daughter and her boyfriend. "Amanda's never brought anyone to meet us," he said pleasantly. "I never knew whether she was ashamed of her boyfriends or of us. I rather think it was us."

Sam, who could not tell from his tone of voice if this was to be taken seriously or not, smiled and said nothing.

"Dad," Amanda said, impatient and uncomfortable, "I don't think Sam wants to hear about that."

Mr. Easton's eyes flashed. "My guess is that there's nothing he would rather hear about." But he looked at Amanda and softened. "I hear you're from Ohio," he said, turning back to Sam.

"Yes sir."

"Nice state. I always liked Ohio."

"When were you ever in Ohio?" Amanda asked skeptically.

Mr. Easton laughed and shrugged his shoulders. He had never understood this emphasis on facts. "What a stickler," he said. "But if you must know, I took a little trip there just last year."

"Business or pleasure or don't you remember?"

"I'm sure dinner is ready," Mrs. Easton said, standing up. "Why don't we go into the dining room?"

The long oak table was set with a simple bone china and the high-backed chairs were placed far apart. The walls were painted a deep matte rust and two of the chandelier's six lights were out—they would have had to squint but for the last squares of daylight coming in through the windows. Mrs. Easton served small portions of a roast chicken that had been cooked earlier that day by the housekeeper and was now tepid and limp.

"It's delicious," Sam said, smiling and chewing at the same time.

Mrs. Easton nodded and they all continued eating. None of the questions Sam had been expecting came up—what do you do for a living, what are your plans, where did you go to school—he wasn't even sure if they knew that he and Amanda were living together. There was only a desultory conversation about the news of the day, some mention of the neighbors' new Irish setter, the renovations in the park—all muted as if someone was asleep in the next room.

"I do think they should leave well enough alone," Mr. Easton said. Sam was nodding in agreement when he noticed Amanda stick her forefinger in her father's glass and raise it to her mouth.

Mr. Easton followed his eyes. "I told you it was soda," he said good-humoredly to Amanda. She removed her finger and wiped it on her napkin.

"I don't know," Mrs. Easton said. "I think some of the new gardens are quite lovely."

Coffee was served back in the living room and as the four of them seemed to have run out of things to talk about, they sat in a silence disturbed only by the faint sound of nylon against nylon as Mrs. Easton crossed her legs. Sam thought of his own family, of the constant noise of his parents' house, the noise he thought all families could not help but make.

And he thought too of the porcelain figurines above the sink in his mother's kitchen back in Ohio, the little boy, his blue overalls chipped and his smile half gone, his fishing pole cast forever into an imaginary lake.

The mannequins with their hard ivory swan necks soaring out of perfectly cut coats of velvet and fur, together or solo, needing no one, acknowledging no one. The darkly lit rooms where even the air itself was still, timeless, cold.

Amanda made one more round of the costume exhibit, waiting for Nancy. She didn't take notes, didn't sketch or read the laminated cards to see who had worn the dresses and how they were made, she was content to walk back and forth, soothed by the glacial elegance.

"Now that's a small waist." Amanda heard Nancy coming up behind her. "Sorry I'm late. Christ. What do you think those women did, use a hammer and a chisel?"

Amanda laughed and kissed Nancy hello. "I heard they had their bottom ribs removed."

"Now that's something to consider. Maybe we should offer some sort of incentive at Legacies. Buy three dresses and we'll throw in a consultation with a plastic surgeon."

"Buy four and we'll do it ourselves in the back room."

Amanda began to follow impatiently after Nancy as she looked at the exhibit, stopping to read every card, exclaiming over a certain trim, a row of velvet bows that Amanda hadn't noticed.

"Okay, okay," Nancy said. "I get the idea. Let's go."

"Coffee or a drink?" Amanda asked as they headed out of the squat cement box of the Fashion Institute.

"Are you kidding? This is the first time I've been out of the house in days. Definitely a drink."

They sat at the bar of a large deserted restaurant where the bubble gum lights bathed their cheeks in a soft pink glow.

"So how's Deirdre working out?" Nancy asked as they waited for the drinks. "I haven't gotten an update from you lately."

Amanda unconsciously straightened her spine, lowered her eyes. "Fine."

"She reminds me of a cheerleader on LSD."

"Look Nancy, you told me I could hire whoever I wanted."

The bartender brought their drinks and then propped up his leg between them, looking for an opening in their conversation. They both glared at him and waited until he walked back over to the service station where a couple of waitresses, their black bow ties hanging undone about their white shirts, were slicing lemons.

"She's just enthusiastic," Amanda said.

"Yeah. But about what?"

"I thought I was supposed to be the closed-minded one. As a matter of fact, she's great with customers."

Nancy smiled. "Okay." She took a sip of her drink. "Anyway, I'm going to start coming in mornings next week."

"You're kidding me?"

"I told you I would as soon as I could find someone to take care of Ben. It'll just be for about four hours a day."

"Good." Amanda smiled. "I mean, it's good you're coming back to work."

They both played with their stirrers.

"So how did it go with your family?" Nancy asked.

"Oh great. My mother's decided that my father was never gone, my father's decided that he was never an alcoholic, and Sam decided that we're all bonkers."

"Did he divorce what's-her-name, Joan?"

"Poor Joan. I don't know. While Sam was trying

41

desperately to chat up my mother in the kitchen, my father showed me a needlepoint pillow she sent him with the AA logo embroidered in.''

"She sent it to your mother's house?''

Amanda shrugged. "You know what they say, love has no pride.'' She took a long sip of her drink and thought about a cigarette, at home between her fingers. "Actually,'' she went on, "Sam handled it really well. He had that wide-eyed gol-lee look on his face, but the Prince Charming act was a big success.'' She motioned to the bartender for another round. "Sometimes I think he's at his best when he's examining odd specimens.''

"What's that mean?''

Amanda smiled. "I don't know. Nothing.''

"Well I think it's that wide-eyed gol-lee look that you love.''

Amanda laughed. "You're right. That's part of it, anyway.'' The air-conditioning was turned up too high and she rubbed her bare arms. "How much did you tell Jack about your past before you married him?''

Nancy laughed. "What past? We were seventeen when we met. Why?''

"I don't know. Sam and I never talk much about it, but . . .''

"Of course not,'' Nancy interrupted.

Amanda looked at her and frowned. "It's not just me, you know. Beneath that Boy Wonder smile of his, he's just as allergic to questions as I am.''

"Okay, look. He knows you weren't exactly a virgin, right?''

"Right. But it's not just that. It's, I don't know . . . Forget it.''

"Well, I guess I should get going,'' Nancy said, pushing aside her full glass. "Jack promised me he'd try to leave the office early tonight. Motherhood doesn't exactly do wonders for a girl's sex life. You don't mind, do you?''

"No. Go ahead. I think I'll stay and finish my drink.''

"Okay," Nancy said as she put some money down on the bar. As she gathered her things into her straw bag she added, "Why don't you and Sam come over for dinner this weekend?"

"Why? You have a prepared dossier on me you want to give him?"

"Actually, I thought I'd slip some sodium pentothal into your wine. It's a dirty job, but someone's got to do it."

Amanda laughed. "Okay. Saturday?"

"Saturday. One last thing, Amanda."

"Yes?"

"I'm sure Sam has some embarrassing skeletons in his closet too."

"Yeah, but they're all probably clean and well pressed."

"What are yours wearing, black leather?"

"Go home and attack your husband."

Amanda drank the rest of her wine slowly. At times the very steadiness, the very certainty that drew her to Sam like a new and curious solvent seemed like a warning—there are limits—and she wondered how she would ever be able to explain the years of yeses to him, the running, wondered if he could ever understand.

Amanda had thought before she met Sam that she could only really want, really desire, dangerous men. But Sam wasn't dangerous, not like that. Only loving him made him the most dangerous of all.

She looked up suddenly and realized that her drink was gone and the bar was filling up with fashion students from the nearby Institute in outfits chic and clashing. It took her ten minutes to pry the bartender away from his audience to total up her bill.

O utside, the heat clung like wet rags, like mud. As she slowly started walking home, Amanda lost her feet, her mind, her sight in the thick cotton gauze. Dizzy, she stopped at a corner where some children were darting through a fire hydrant's steady gusts of water and smiled at a little girl who stood alone to the side, her hands folded across her round belly, her hair done up in a myriad of colorful barrettes. "Great hairdo," Amanda said. The girl stared, silent and serious, and then she ran suddenly through the water. Dripping now, she smiled shyly back at Amanda. Amanda waved and started walking.

She was about four blocks from her apartment, lost once more to the octopus haze, when she looked up and spotted the familiar shape of Sam's back, his broad shoulders, the white shirt that she had worn the day before, his slightly pigeon-toed walk, boyish and sweet, just a few yards away. It smacked through, the surprise of knowing just where this man was going, of knowing that there was a coffee stain on his shirttail that she had left behind, of knowing how he made love, it smacked through and suddenly nothing else mattered, nothing but this knowing and this slightly pigeon-toed walk, boyish and sweet, cracking her heart and re-forming it with every step. She forgot herself, forgot everything but them, and started to run giddily toward him, this man, Sam, slowing to a more casual pace when she was almost by his side.

"Going my way, sailor?"

Sam started and then turned quickly around. "Maybe."

Pieces of blue shot out of his eyes like broken crystal. "How much?"

"Make me an offer."

He stood back and looked her up and down, he was smiling still. "Four ninety-nine."

"Talk about your cheap dates."

They both laughed and Sam leaned over and kissed her cheek, soft and salty. "Hi."

"Hi."

They fell automatically to walking home together and though they pretended to take it for granted, it was still new enough, unexpected enough—home together—to warrant some sort of remark.

"Why don't we have dinner up on the roof?" Amanda suggested.

"I didn't know you could go up there."

"Well you're not supposed to, but it'll be okay if we're careful."

"You sure?"

Amanda laughed. "Can I ask you a personal question?"

"I doubt it. But go ahead, try."

"Were you ever a Boy Scout?"

He smiled. "You're such a little snob. But yes, as a matter of fact, I was."

Amanda smiled too. "It's okay. I'm a sucker for a man in uniform."

"I bet."

Like burglars, they cautiously pried open the musty door to the roof, clumsily balancing their sandwiches and beers, and tiptoed onto the steaming black cushions of tar. Amanda spread out an old down sleeping bag while Sam walked over to the ledge and scanned the view. Uptown, the mirror and cement spires rose with stubborn pride through the thick sky and shimmered in the day's last light—but they were far away and had nothing to do with them. He turned his back on them, on this city that would encircle them with its vanities and its accomplishments, they didn't need it, not tonight. A few feet away, Amanda was resting on her elbows, her eyes closed and her face held up to the sky as if waiting for a promise, and it touched him more than all town's lit-up avenues. He took a deep breath before moving toward her, but even here the air was smouldering and dense—there would be no relief this evening.

"You owe me," he said as he sat down beside her. He took a long sip of the beer that she offered him and wiped his mouth with the back of his hand.

"Owe you what?"

"A personal question."

Amanda smiled. "Ask me anything. My life is an open book."

"In what, Sanskrit?"

She flinched and glanced quickly away. His sarcasm was always a surprise to her, unexpected, disturbing, knocking off guard everything she presumed and tipping the scales in favor of reconsideration. She dipped her finger into a glistening dot of tar and wiped it on the ragged heel of her sandal. She knew too that it was the impatient way he cut through that she needed. "No," she said, smiling, "I was never a cheerleader."

Sam waited. The muted music of the street was far, far below them, like a threadbare carpet of car horns and radios. "Are you happy?" he asked quietly.

Amanda frowned. "Some question."

"Well?"

She reached over and took the crease of his chinos between her fingers, moving up and down along its faded line, up and down, her eyes never quite getting above his knee, there was only this crease. She gave it a final wistful tug before releasing it. "I love you," she said gently when she could finally look into his eyes.

Sam smiled, it wasn't what he had asked. Nevertheless, his hand moved to her hip, to the crescent beneath the thin cotton of her dress where the bone left the flesh behind—it was his place and his alone, and sometimes he was content just to rest his lips there, reveling in his discovery. He leaned over, finding it, reclaiming it . . .

Amanda looked down at the top of Sam's head, golden in the waning light, it made her bite her lip, cringe, this lovely sunset head of his, and she bent slowly over it, lower, nuzzling the moist back of his neck with her mouth, surely she had found a home in its hollow, yes, and they sank together onto the lumpy roof. They did not kiss but seemed to roll into each other with an almost resigned lassitude, as if diving into the heat itself, removing what bits of clothing they could, unpeeling, searching, here. Despite a growing urgency though—here, yes here—their bodies quickly grew so slick and sweaty that they could not get a firm grasp but seemed to slide off of each other instead.

The cologne bottle was shaped like a penis and Sam moved it this way and that on the page, trying to avoid making a statement with its position. Sideways or up or down, it slanted the meaning of the copy into drifts he did not want. It was still early and the office had the graying stillness of an empty eggshell and the high heels quickly clicking down the hall only gradually made their way inside Sam's consciousness. The woman was at his desk before he had a chance to look up.

"Are you in charge here?" She poised her long salmon-colored nails on a stack of cut-up sentences. Sam put his hands over the layout and looked at her, caught by her skin turned orange from the sun, and then he glanced about the empty room.

"I guess so," he said. "Is there a problem?"

The woman smiled. "No problem. I'm Miriam Yatnikoff from Lacey's Lingerie down the hall. I just thought it was time I came over and said hello. See what you folks are up to in here." She flipped a wedge of stiff ash blonde hair off of her thin shoulder.

Sam returned her smile. "We're a magazine."

Mrs. Yatnikoff scanned the walls, covered with black-and-white blowups of runway models, their bodies distorted, their clothes obscured by the tangled camera angles. "I like it," she murmured. "I like it. It's very artistic, isn't it?"

Sam nodded.

Just then, Patrick walked into the office and Mrs.

Yatnikoff instinctively stood up straighter and shot a wide stretch of smile in his direction. "I'd better get back to work," she whispered.

Sam said good-bye and waited until she was out of the door before taking his hands off of the phallic cutout.

Later that day, Patrick called Sam into his office. "Who was that woman with the hair?" he asked.

"Mrs. Yatnikoff from Lacey's Lingerie," he answered.

Patrick bounced this up and down like a colorful beach ball. "Maybe she could model some of her company's things for us," he said.

Sam smiled half-heartedly. It was just the kind of thing that *Backlog* did, tongue in someone else's cheek, and he wanted to push it back, to say No, she's a nice lady, leave her alone, don't make fun of her. But of course, he had no proof that they were making fun of her, and besides, he had been here long enough to suspect that there was nothing Mrs. Yatnikoff would like quite so much as having her picture in *Backlog*.

"Ask her," Patrick said as he reached to answer the flat pale green phone that was blinking soundlessly on his desk.

"Okay."

"By the way," he continued, cradling the receiver by his ear, "your friend Mark is coming in later. What do you know about his last project?"

"Nothing."

Patrick nodded and turned his attention to his caller, a minor countess visiting from Spain, and Sam left the room.

That evening, he waited for Mark and the two of them left the building together.

"What was that all about?" Sam asked as they started walking downtown together.

Mark laughed. "Patrick wanted the dirt on that movie I did in D.C. last month. He's trying to figure out if it's going to be the underground breakthrough sleeper hit of the year or just another of my B-side flops. You want to go have a beer?"

"Sure."

"Good. To tell you the truth, the only reason I agreed to come in was because I wanted to see you."

"I'm honored. Why?"

"To reminisce about the good ole days in Allensville."

Sam laughed. Their days in Allensville had skirted each other, for Mark had always been going in a faster spiral, farther and farther out, had always pressed for more—and then left, while Sam held to the center, held on and watched, fascinated, secretly envious, watched and tried to unearth the source of Mark's simple confidence. Even now Sam had a habit of hanging back and observing how Mark walked, how he spoke, thinking that perhaps he would finally discover the riddle of his assurance.

"No," Mark said, as he aimed them into a crowded bar, "what I really want to talk to you about is a proposal I have." He got lost for a minute in the exaggerated curves of a redhead on her way to the ladies' room. "Anyway," he came back to Sam, "I've been talking to a couple of people I know, money people, about this treatment. Everyone agrees it would make a great screenplay."

Sam took a sip of his draft and got a mouth full of foam. "I didn't know you wrote."

"I don't. That's where you come in."

Sam laughed. "I don't know a goddam thing about writing screenplays. I've never even seen one before."

"Will you hear me out at least? Jesus. First of all, you can read a few and see how they're done. It's no big deal. Second of all, I remember those short stories you published a couple of years ago in Allensville."

Sam squirmed on his bar stool. He had never mentioned them to a soul in New York, they were a hidden litter of runts that he had tried to forget the minute he left them behind, where they belonged, in the basket of earlier years.

"Despite what I know you think," Mark continued, "I always liked them. I never understood why you stopped. I mean, you can't really like putting together a magazine for fashion victims."

"I made a grand total of one hundred and seventy-five dollars for my so-called creative work," Sam said drily. "Besides, that was a long time ago."

"Okay. Anyway, I still think you'd be perfect for this."

"Perfect for what?"

"For collaborating with me on the screenplay."

"Oh c'mon. You must know a hundred other people better suited for that."

"A hundred and two, but I can't afford any of them. Besides, I think we'd work well together and it would get you out of that chi-chi hellhole you insist on calling a career."

Sam laughed. "It's not that bad."

"Right. Anyway, will you do me a favor and just read the outline before you give me a decision?" He pulled a tattered manila envelope from his knapsack and placed it next to Sam.

Sam fingered the corners as he watched it slide closer. "Is there a part in it for Mrs. Yatnikoff?"

"Huh?"

"Nothing."

"Look, I don't want to talk about plot or characterization until you've had a chance to think about it, but I do want you to know that I'm completely open to ideas."

"Okay." Sam finished the rest of his beer in one gulp. "So," he said, looking directly at Mark for the first time in five minutes, "you think the Mets stand a chance of pulling it out?"

S he could feel it, could feel the touch he gave now to the baby nestled on his lap, soft and downy and new, as if his hands were inside the walls of her stomach pushing out, could feel it squeeze her heart between his fingers, tighter, closer, so that she had to rebel against it or strangle in its clutch.

"Careful, Captain Kangaroo," Amanda warned. "He's about to knock over your drink."

Sam shifted the baby from one knee to the other and continued bouncing him gently up and down while tiny bubbles of pleasure spilled from his little red mouth.

"Don't let him get too excited," Nancy called from the open kitchen. "I want to try to get him to sleep before we eat."

Jack rolled his eyes.

"Well I can dream, can't I?" Nancy came out of the kitchen carrying a plate of homemade pâté and pushed aside the baby bottle and a couple of Jack's law books with her spare hand before settling it down. Amanda watched as she lifted Ben from Sam's lap and held him up in the air, wriggling him about and grinning up into his happy face, she watched her kiss him, the fluidity of it—it's natural, isn't it? baby, husband, dinner, easy and natural, why not?—and it filled her up with a clanging discomfort that she could not quite place. She frowned unconsciously as she recrossed her legs and reached for her wine. Sam put his hand on her lap and she smiled distractedly at him.

"So," Jack said as he turned to Sam, "I just read an article about *Backlog* in the business section. Your advertising pages are up twenty-four percent?"

"So it seems."

Amanda turned to him. "You didn't tell me that."

"I guess I forgot. Anyway, I'm on the editorial end. I try to ignore all that nonsense."

"Not me," Nancy said, laughing. "I'd have asked for a raise the next day."

"Money's not what's lacking over there. It's brains. I ask for more pages, they give them to shoe manufacturers."

"Art versus commerce, so what else is new?" Jack said.

"I'm not sure we should bring art into this," Sam said. "I mean, why start now?" He laughed and took a sip of his drink. "Anyway, I have a few things I'm trying to slip in through the back door, but I can think of more pleasant topics of conversation."

"Well while you think," Nancy said, "I'm going to go try to get Ben to sleep."

When they sat down to eat at the dining room table a few minutes later, they could still hear the baby whimpering his way softly into his own baby twilight and Jack and Nancy ate quickly, pretending not to listen.

"He had to have his head measured the other day," Jack said between mouthfuls of pasta. "That's what they do now, they measure heads. You think they did that to us?"

"What do they do if it's the wrong size?" Sam asked.

"Send them to Hollywood," Amanda suggested.

"Actually, I don't know what it's for. All I know is that his head was the right size."

"To say nothing of his lungs," Nancy added. "I think I've had a migraine since the day he was born."

"So are you two going to take a vacation?" Jack asked.

"Careful, don't give my partner any funny ideas.

53

There'll be no vacations until Ben is in graduate school. I thought that was understood."

Amanda hardly smiled.

"Anyway," Sam said, glancing away from her to Jack, "I've been reading about you in the papers too. That case you're trying for the city. Did that creep really try to bribe the judge?"

Jack smiled. "The surprising part is he got caught. Didn't you used to cover courtrooms?"

Sam laughed. "In Allensville? Sure. But a heavy crime was when someone pocketed a package of saltines from the Safeway."

"Honey, tell them what the guy said when the judge reported it." Nancy's hand was on Jack's, prodding, pulling. "You're not going to believe this," she said, laughing as she kissed him.

Amanda was watching it, watching this in out, unrolling like a spool of film, in out ours, so easy at her feet, this melding in out, she was watching how it worked with a new curiosity that jangled up her stomach, in out ours, easy and natural, why not? She squinted her eyes and watched closely, hardly catching a word of Jack's description of the seven-hundred-dollar suits delivered to back doors and the chauffeurs with their attachés of cash.

She was still quietly watching it when Nancy and Jack both began to yawn over their coffee and Sam suggested that they leave. "It's a school night, after all," he said.

Outside, Amanda began to cut through the street like a storm, he had seen it before, this fast too fast walk whenever there was some kind of trouble inside. Her heels slapped stubbornly at the pavement and he forced himself to catch up with her.

"Is something wrong?" Sam asked. "You were so quiet tonight."

"Nothing's wrong." Her voice was as impatient as her feet. "I just didn't feel like talking."

"Okay," he said under his breath, "next." He quickened his pace, trying to find her. "It was fun playing with Ben. You think we'll be good parents?" It was so light, it was almost a game.

"How should I know?" Amanda snapped.

Neither of them knew what it was, there was no proof, only this nervous stutter of a walk.

Amanda left Sam up front to lock up while she went into the bathroom and scoured her face, her hands, her neck, cleaner and cleaner still, there was no place left to walk to, no place left to go, she could only scrub herself, cleaner and cleaner, taking off her earrings, her necklace, cleaner, while Sam sat on the bed and waited for her.

But it was still there when she crawled beneath the sheets, still there, pushing, revving, poking, and she lay with her fists clenched tightly, no place to go, tightly beneath her, squeezing and squeezing, clenched so tight that by the time Sam came back from brushing his teeth and climbed in beside her, her arms were already beginning to grow numb—he lay on his back, still, his arms by his sides—and she began to know now, finally, what she had been clutching so tightly all those nights when her arms had grown numb as ice—it was the wanting. It was the wanting she had never felt before, not really, the wanting that until now had been safe and distant and abstract, she had always made sure of that, the wanting that had always been as untouchable as the moon and now had a form, a body, a smell and a touch, it was the wanting that she would squeeze out of her.

Sam turned over, lay with his back to her.

She took a deep breath and opened her hands, slowly, finger by finger, there was nothing left to do, for she knew that it was hers now, this wanting, and she could not squeeze it away, it was hers and it would not go away. Tears began to form in the corners of her eyes.

"Sam?" She touched his arm and he rolled over onto his back and looked at her. "I'm sorry."

"For what?" He wanted facts.

"It's not easy for me."

"What's not?"

"This, all of it, even talking about it, us."

He pulled her head over to his shoulder. "I know."

"Isn't it hard for you?"

"Of course it is. But sometimes I think you fight it too much. What are you so scared of?"

"I don't know."

An ambulance screeched past and they waited until its alarm faded into the night.

"Amanda?"

"Yes?"

"I'm not going anyplace."

"You're not?"

"No."

"Me neither."

The tears had left her eyes and she was crying softly, softly with the giving up of it, the giving in to it, the wanting that was hers, that had a form, that held her in its arms, not quite as untouchable as the moon.

"You think we can pull it off?" she asked quietly.

Sam smiled. "You make it sound like a scam."

She smiled too and kissed him and he said, "Yes, I think we can," and she heard herself say, "Yes, I think so too," and she could feel it, inside the walls of her stomach, pushing out.

"So you think they're going to get married, you know, with a ceremony, the whole shebang?" Sally leaned forward across the yellow tablecloth and asked in her usual breathless manner.

"Maybe they'll just live in sin," Amanda said, looking around for a waiter.

Sally and Amanda had recently pried themselves into the habit of having lunch together once a week. It had begun when Mrs. Easton was alone, obstinately refusing to leave her apartment, and the two sisters had formed a temporary alliance to search for a remedy. Now they attempted to continue the meetings, though it was an unstated rule that either could cancel at a moment's notice and one of them often did.

"I still don't see why you won't go see them," Amanda said.

"Frank's against the idea. And anyway, I told you, I think Mom was a fool to take him back."

"Well that's her decision, isn't it?"

"That doesn't mean I have to agree with it." Sally's voice took on a vehemence that existed only for her father, for if Amanda had decided early on to step carefully out of his way and barely show a raised eyebrow when he tripped, Sally had spent too many years tugging at his sleeve, pleading, cajoling, crying, until she had finally turned her back on him.

Amanda looked at her coolly for a moment. "How's

Frank?'' she asked. It sounded like a challenge, perhaps it was.

"Well despite how things might have seemed at dinner that night, we're on a pretty even keel at the moment." Sally drained her piña colada. "You seem to bring out the worst in him."

"It's not hard."

"Look, at least he's not bugging me about having another kid." The left side of her mouth sank. "He just sits at his desk all day thinking up little projects for me and cutting out pieces of the latest psychobabble to leave on the refrigerator door." Sally laughed. "He's into home improvement."

Amanda smiled. It was only recently that Sally had shown any irony when referring to her marriage, and if at times it shot out a little too harshly, it was still better than the sanctimonious defense that had preceded it. "I just don't see why you don't leave him if you're so unhappy."

"You don't see a lot of things," Sally snapped.

They both paused to order the Hawaiian salad from the waiter who had been hovering above them.

"What's that supposed to mean?" Amanda asked when he had left their table.

"It means that it's not that simple. In case you've forgotten, I have a daughter to think of. And Frank's a good father. Besides, you might not understand this, but I happen to like being married." She rubbed a waterspot off her fork. "Things will be better when I get a job."

"You've been saying you're going to get a job for over a year now."

"Well, I haven't found what I'm looking for."

"There's no such thing as nine-to-five salvation."

"How would you know? You've never stuck with anything in your life."

"Maybe that's why. Besides, I've decided to stay with Legacies."

"Let's just forget it."

Their salads arrived in large clay pineapple halves and they busied themselves with cutting them up for a minute.

"So," Sally said, pushing aside a hairy piece of coconut shell, "whatever happened to Bill?"

"I see him now and then."

"Figures."

"I'm not sleeping with him, if that's what you mean."

"You mean you're actually being faithful?"

"Yes, Sally."

Sally considered this for a moment, weighing, measuring, ascertaining whether their stabs were equal. Whatever her decision, she smiled and let it go. "It's not all it's cracked up to be," she said.

"What's not?"

"Fidelity."

Amanda laughed. "My, my, things have changed."

"I'm just kidding. You know that."

"I know."

"I mean, I never have, I never would . . . Well, maybe, I don't know . . ."

"Look Sally, the thing about Bill was it was never just about sex."

"You mean you were only holding hands all these years?"

Amanda smiled. "Holding something."

"But you were never really with him. It always seemed like a five-year one-night stand to me."

"More than five years. I don't know. We're friends. We're a lot alike. Or were, anyway."

"How are you like him?"

"You might not understand this, but I think we both saw any form of settling down as kind of, what?, as giving in, I guess. No, that's not it. Maybe we're both just scared of stopping, of quiet." Amanda smiled. "That's not it either. You were right. It had to do with great sex."

"Well, what made you change your mind?"

"I don't know. Maybe it's just the way Sam looks at me. He's so goddam sincere. I guess I like that."

"For you that constitutes an all-out breast-beating declaration."

"I'm flat-chested enough without breast-beating."

"Should we have another drink?"

"I can't, Sally. I need to get back to work."

Sally looked down at the remains of her salad.

"Look, Sally, if I can do anything to help . . ."

"Help what? What makes you think I need your help?"

"I only mean that if you want the store to fake you a recommendation, something like that."

"Thanks. Look, why don't you go ahead if you want. It's my turn to pay anyway."

"That's all right."

They played with their napkins while they waited for the check.

"So how was he?" Sally asked.

"Who?"

"Dad."

"He was fine. Sober."

"Temporarily."

Amanda shrugged. "He really wants to see you."

The check came and Sally got out her wallet. "Maybe."

The shooting with Mrs. Yatnikoff had been going on
for a good two hours. Sam, who was supposed to be
supervising the proceedings, sat perched on top of a desk
cluttered with shiny nylon lingerie in cardboard boxes,
trying to remain as unobtrusive as possible.

"That's it," the photographer enthused. "That's it,
now just tip your head back a tad . . . sultry, give me
sultry . . . that's it, perfect . . . now just a little smile,
that's it, just a soupçon . . ."

While the stylist rearranged the black peignoir and
the photographer reloaded her camera, Mrs. Yatnikoff
winked a heavily lashed eye over at Sam and Sam smiled
back and quickly looked away. There were still five outfits
to go.

When he finally got home after eight o'clock that
night, Sam paced back and forth in the living room,
pulling at his hair, biting his lip. "You wouldn't believe
what a load of assholes they were," he sputtered to
Amanda. "At the end, they did this double-kiss routine
and she laps it up while they go on and on about her
cover girl potential. Christ, I hate that place."

Amanda watched as Sam pulled up a chair beside
her at the table. The grooves in his face fanned out into a
semicircle from his eyes down to his mouth, deep and
resolute. His anger seemed too big, too hard to her, as if
he were being threatened by a knife-wielding gang and
his only hope was to scream his way out of it. Or perhaps
their crime was simply assuming that he was one of them?

She remembered how he had once talked about reporting, in the beginning, when his eyes would hold his hopes like a candle. It was one of the things that first drew her to him, held her, it was what was fine and good—for she had never found anything to care about in quite that way and she regarded it as a curious and lovely bauble, to be treasured.

"Maybe you should just quit," she said tentatively. To be treasured, protected, fed. "Find something better."

"Have you forgotten what a hard time I had finding a job the last time? I can't just quit." The simplicity of her suggestion belied—among other things—a cushion of family money, where he had known only a long skein of loans, rents, debts. "I can't just quit," he repeated as he distractedly reached for a pile of junk mail from the corner. Amanda watched as he leafed through a hardware catalog, scowling at the saws and the workbenches.

"Will you give me half an hour?" she asked.

"What?"

She smiled at him. "Put your life in my hands for half an hour."

"I'm not in the mood," Sam said.

"That's not what I mean. Just follow me, okay?"

He pushed away the catalog. "Okay."

Amanda deposited Sam in a warm bubble bath brimming with apricot-scented bubbles. She turned off the lights on her way out of the bathroom and returned a minute later with a brandy.

"Here," she said, handing it to him.

Sam smiled. "Care to join me?"

"No. You have strict orders to stay in here until you're less cranky."

He laughed. "Yes ma'am."

Sam dunked his head beneath the water and let the warmth seep in through his scalp, coddling the serrated edges, the raw skin. He took a deep breath of steam and rose, stretching the length of the tub and taking a sip of brandy, holding it on his tongue for a moment before letting it slip down, heat inside of heat. Slowly, it began to melt away, Patrick's perpetual amusement, the phallic layouts, the copy he had written that would never be quite right, that would never be his. He slicked his hair off of his forehead. Buried beneath a pile of T-shirts in the back of a drawer lay Mark's treatment, unread, unmentioned, nagging and teasing and whispering like an unswallowed pill being saved for another time, a worse time, a better time, he didn't know. He took another sip of brandy and as it hit his stomach he got a momentary image of Mrs. Yatnikoff's sultry pout and he laughed out loud and then listened as it resonated in the dark tiled room and slowly drifted off. The bubbles had flattened into a pale gray foam and he began to squiggle imaginary equations into it with his forefinger, open-ended equations, equations with no answers, only variables, that collided, that mocked, that canceled each other out, equation atop equation, melting in the foam, but all he could see, all he could come up with was this: Amanda. With her impulsive solutions that he wanted only to believe in, with her blind spots that kept her from seeing the shaking in his legs, with her smoke screens and her perfume and her sad little smile.

When Sam emerged thirty minutes later, calm, fragrant, he walked into the bedroom, turned down the volume of the television movie Amanda was watching, and sat down on the bed beside her.

"Will you marry me?" he asked, smiling.

Amanda laughed and wiped a wet strand of hair off of his forehead. "Feeling better, are we?"

Sam put his hand on hers. "I mean it," he said. "Will you marry me?"

"I know a bubble bath can work miracles, but this is ridiculous."

"Amanda."

63

She looked down at his hand, soft and puckered still. "Ask me in the morning," she said.

"What's wrong with now?"

"Now you're all warm and pampered and it wouldn't count."

"You mean I have to be cold and hung over and cranky to propose to you?"

"Yes."

"Okay. I will."

But when Sam woke the next morning, Amanda had already left for work. He looked over at the glowing orange digits of the clock and realized that for the first time in months, he had overslept.

When Amanda reached the block that Legacies was on, she saw Nancy kneeling in the window, arranging a trio of blue and white antique silk kimonos.

She put the heavy ring of keys that she had been using to open up back in her bag and smiled as she went in. "Welcome back."

"Thanks." Nancy continued to pin the wide sleeves so that the fabric hung perpendicular to the floor and the intricate butterfly patterns could be seen from the street. When she was done, she stood up, placed three black boater hats where heads were supposed to be and then climbed carefully out of the window.

Amanda walked into the back room and dropped her bag down on the old rolltop desk that had been hers for the last six months before she realized that Nancy's things were already settled there.

"I'll move my stuff," Nancy said as she entered the room behind her. She still had a long row of pins attached to her blouse.

"Don't worry about it."

"Well maybe I'll go out later and buy another desk. I just need a small one. I'm still going to do most of my work from home."

"Okay."

"So," Nancy said, "let's see some of the new things. The Polaroids I've been looking at leave something to be desired."

"Most things do."

"Uh oh. Something wrong."

"No. Here," Amanda said, leading Nancy to a group of thin knit skirts, white on white, black on black, the faint triangular patterns barely visible. "What do you think?"

Nancy sighed sadly.

"You don't like them?"

"No, I love them. I was just thinking that I'll never be able to wear anything like that again."

"Don't be ridiculous. You look terrific."

"Let's not kid ourselves. Even my knees have stretch marks. Not that I ever have an excuse for getting dressed up these days. Anyway, they're great. Are they the models you said were moving so quickly?"

"Yeah. I put an order in for another dozen."

"That's terrific. What else should I see?"

After they had made the rounds of the small store, Amanda went in the back to finish up some paperwork from the day before and Nancy stayed up front, keeping her eye on Deirdre, picking up miniscule pieces of lint from the geometric rug, removing a couple of wilting petals from the large flower arrangement on the counter, rolling and rerolling the sleeves of a fuchsia sweater.

When lunchtime came, she went in the back and ate with Amanda.

"Maybe I was wrong about Deirdre," she said. "She seems to be handling things pretty well."

Amanda nodded and pushed her take-out salad about with a small plastic fork. "So listen," she said matter-of-factly, "I think Sam asked me to marry him."

Nancy stared at her in disbelief. "Are you kidding me? You waited till now to tell me? I don't believe it. Tell me everything. What did he say? What did you say? What do you mean, you think, anyway?"

"Well, he said, 'Will you marry me?' and I said, 'Ask me in the morning,' and he didn't."

"Why did you tell him to ask you again?"

"I don't know. Maybe he didn't mean it. You know, temporary insanity."

"Your confidence is overwhelming." Nancy sucked some iced tea through her straw. "Do you want to marry him?"

"I don't know."

"I thought you loved him."

"I do love him. I'm just not that sure of marriage. Christ, you and Jack are the only people I know who make it work."

"What makes you think you couldn't make it work?"

"How long have you got?"

"I'm serious."

"So am I." Amanda looked up, shrugged, looked down. "Marriage is just one of those things I never thought I'd do. I don't know. Christ, I never even had a steady boyfriend before. Maybe we don't know each other well enough. Maybe we're too different. And anyway," she said, looking once more at Nancy, "he'll probably change his mind. He probably already did."

"Maybe he's waiting for you to say something. Look, Amanda, you're going to have to trust someone sometime. Why not just take the chance?"

Amanda didn't say anything but accidentally broke off one of the tongs of her fork.

They ate the rest of their lunch in silence, but as they were closing up the clear plastic containers of their salads, Amanda asked, "Nancy?"

"Yes?"

"Do you think he'll ask again?" He had left once before, after all, left before, people had a way of disappearing.

"Sure. Anyway, you could always ask him."

Amanda laughed. "Absolutely not."

"Well, I had to ask Jack at least fifteen times before he finally agreed. And I think the butcher knife I was waving had something to do with his answer."

"Weren't you scared?"

"Not as scared as he was."

"No. I mean of marriage. The idea of being tied to someone like that terrifies me."

"I guess the idea of not being tied to someone terrified me more."

They brushed off the desk and collected the rest of their garbage. "I really am glad you're back," Amanda said quietly as she tried to squeeze the containers into the little brass basket.

"Good. Now I'm going to go out and find myself a desk to sit at."

PART TWO

The proposal lay between them, mute, unmentioned. Its outline, lengthening like a shadow at dusk, had wormed its way between them like a third person, a bully. . . .

Sam stood staring out of the window at the traffic stalled at a red light below. The sky was the deep oyster gray of early evening and the headlights shone through like soft milky white beams. He hadn't exactly planned on asking her to marry him, not then anyway, not like that. But he knew as soon as he had said it that it was what he wanted, needed, to put an end to their fluid courtship, never quite clear enough, never quite solid enough, he knew that he wanted something firmer, something that he could grasp onto and hold as his, he knew that he wanted to marry her. It was time. He was unconscious of his hands, tapping repeatedly on the sooty glass panes. Couldn't she just have said yes?

Amanda was inside dressing for the evening. She still preferred to dress in private, not because of any innate inhibitions about nudity, though there was that too, but because she was embarrassed by her vanities, her insecurities, the putting on, shifting, taking off, switching. She settled at last on a black linen skirt and a lacy thrift-shop blouse and went into the bathroom to blot her lipstick on toilet paper.

When she finally walked out into the living room, Sam was silhouetted in the window, his back to her, remote, implacable, as far away as China. She stood still, chilled, and then, just when she was about to go up to him, to put her arms around him, he turned suddenly around, and she flinched instead.

"Ready?" he asked.

"I just have to get my bag."

As they walked in the direction of the restaurant where *Backlog* was holding its monthly publication party, the sounds of their feet hitting the pavement in unison sounded as a reproach to them both. Sam took Amanda's hand.

"I'm sorry I overslept the other day," he said. "I really did mean it though. I want to marry you."

Her muscles tensed, relieved, not relieved . . . they kept on walking. . . .

"Say something," Sam implored.

"I don't know what to say. I'm not sure I'm ready to get married."

"You're thirty years old. When do you plan on being ready?" And then, "Sorry."

"Look, I didn't say no. Can't we talk about it later?"

They had reached the ornately carved wooden door of the restaurant. As Sam held it open for her, he said, "Okay, later," and they found themselves inside of the noisy party, pulled by faces familiar and unknown away from each other. Sam left Amanda at the bar talking animatedly to Deirdre and he went to get something to eat.

"Come with me," Patrick said, pulling Sam away from the crowded hors d'oeuvres table before he had even found a plate. "There are some potential advertisers I want you to chat up." He found himself deposited into a spinning orb of avant-garde shoe designers, restaurant reps and mystical bookstore owners, spewing page rates and story lines, while Patrick wandered off to the bar.

It took Sam over an hour to extricate himself and find Amanda, who was leaning up against a man he had never seen before and laughing loudly at his jokes. Sam nodded hello and pulled her a half-step away. "Are you ready to leave?" His tolerance was never as high as hers for these affairs, and if tonight she was obviously finding it a refuge, it was more of an irritant to him.

"Sure. I told Peter we'd meet him at the bar around the corner."

"I'd rather not."

"C'mon. It'll be fun."

Sam looked at Amanda and recognized an enlivened glow that he had seen once or twice before, when the night, its rhythms and its chatter, its swirling neon dervishes, appeared to enter her, filling her up with an insistent energy that seemed to carry her willfully away from him.

"You go," he said. "I'm tired."

"You sure you don't mind?" Her gaze had wandered to the door—she was there already, around the corner, away from him.

"No. Go ahead. I'll see you later." He kissed her good-bye and left.

The bar was one Amanda used to frequent, handing out her hours to a parade of people in the dark red and black upstairs room, but it had faded from her mind during the well-lit nights of moderation she spent with Sam, it was stashed away with other fragments, other secrets. It surprised her now to find so many of the same people leaning on the tiny tables, receding and reappearing from the same slate smoke, gurgling about what were surely the same lovers' rifts, overrated shows, hopeless quests for lofts. Perhaps it hadn't been as long as she had thought, as far. She ordered a double vodka and joined her friends in a crowded booth, her voice a little louder than usual, her smile a little brighter. "Well," Peter said as he put his arms around her and ruffled up her hair, "if it isn't the return of the prodigal daughter. I thought we'd lost you to the land of sensible shoes and early mornings."

Amanda smiled. "And leave all this behind?"

"They always revert," he explained to the table.

She sat back and tried to blend into the conversation,

it used to be so easy, but it was boiling without her now, and she found herself watching their mouths flap flap flapping like a poorly dubbed movie . . . . *and then when he kicked her out she went back to her old girlfriend's place but she had lost her lease and moved to New Mexico to some art commune and then he called and wanted her to come back but she had already moved in with her father who's in the middle of his third divorce no? yes, and he had found a great apartment* . . . they always revert . . . *and she figured she might as well stay and* . . .

"You have some quarters?" Amanda asked suddenly of no one, everyone.

She took a handful and went over to the jukebox, thrusting her money into the slot—this song and then this one, this is the one, really it is, yes, this one, she rapped her fingers restlessly on the smudged glass, no she should have played that other one, too late, no more money, but that was the one she had really wanted to hear, the one that was so good that it melted in your gut, that was what she meant, well it really didn't matter, it didn't matter at all—she went back to the booth, her legs rattling beneath the table too fast for the beat, her eyes foraging each face as it went by, and they were talking now about who was dying, how many more, how much longer, how come.

She was in a race now, a reckless high-speed race, against something she could not see, but only feel, amorphous, vaguely threatening, within. Amanda drew people to her the way a woman does when she doesn't care—truly does not care—where the night ends as long as it is far away, and she drove into it, laughing, drinking, flirting, drove into it, glittering and determined, head first . . .

In the background, she had noticed Bill and waved to him, was it an hour ago? two? Now he walked over to her table and knelt down beside her.

"You seem to be in fine form tonight," he said, kissing her hello.

"Fine form," Amanda agreed, smiling like a crooked pirate as she held her face up close to his.

But Bill had known Amanda for a long time, had seen the nights of wayward eyes, wayward hands, when without telling anyone she had raised the stakes so high that no one, not even she, could play. "Are you okay?" he asked as he smoothed his hand slowly down her cheek.

"I'm great." Her voice was slurred, syrupy and deep. "What's the matter, don't I look great?"

"You look great. Where's Sam?"

"Sam? Sam is at home, tucked in, sleeping the sleep of the innocent." She had wrapped her leg playfully about his and he had to disengage himself to stand up. "The sleep of the just, the sleep of . . ."

"*Caramba,*" Bill said, rolling his eyes. He slid in next to her. "I haven't seen you like this in a long time."

Amanda shrugged. "Do you remember the bathroom in here?" She had placed her chin on his shoulder, her mouth inside his ear. "Do you think you can still get high if you lick the sink? We used to like that, didn't we? It was fun, wasn't it?" She picked up her head, pulled briefly at her hair. "I think it was fun, I don't remember. Was it fun?"

He kissed her on the cheek. "It was fun. Sure, it was fun."

She smiled sadly. "It used to be so easy to go away, anyplace we wanted, right?, there were so many places to go, it was so easy to disappear, we did it all the time, we did it for years, didn't we?"

"Yeah." Bill took a sip of his beer. "But everyone's gotta pay sometime, I guess."

"Not you, though."

"Not me."

Amanda's eyes began once again to slam hip hop about the room, denser now, smokier, the desperate mumblings of closing time moored up at the tables and the bar.

She watched as a young man who looked vaguely familiar rubbed an ice cube on his date's forehead. "Tell me," she said, turning back to Bill with a beaten-up smile curling her lips, "you're the expert on Dante. What circle do you think this is?"

"Christ, Amanda. It's a bar, just a bar."

She chewed her ice cube obstinately and he looked at her and put down his shoulders. "Okay," he said, knowing, "okay, but not tonight. C'mon," he stood up and began to pull her with him. "Let's get out of here."

"Where are we going?"

"Home."

"But I told you, honey. Sam's at home."

"Exactly."

Bill held her up as they waited for a cab and pushed her in first before sliding down next to her. Suddenly, the insatiable energy that had been rattling through her arteries vanished and she found herself alone, shaken and scared. She buried her face in Bill's shoulder.

"What's the matter?" he asked softly. "What is it?"

"I don't know."

He let her out in front of the door and watched to make sure she got into the building safely before telling the driver to continue.

Upstairs, Sam was waiting anxiously for her, sitting, standing, walking, standing, sitting, waiting. But when he saw what condition she was in, the feelings of concern turned cold and censorious. "Where have you been?" he asked as she stumbled past him into the living room. Her face had shrunk so that her makeup stood out like a smeared Kabuki mask. "It's four in the morning."

Amanda slumped onto the couch. "Drinking, friends," she muttered. But when she looked up at him, her eyes were shining like armor, full of bravado, shining with a challenge. This was it, then, her gauntlet, this was it: Here is my worst self, here, look at this, do you still want me, do you, or will you leave? This was it then, for what she really wanted, needed, was for him to say, again and again and again and again, I am here. Of course, she had only the haziest sense of this now as she added, without apology, "Didn't realize it was so late."

"C'mon," he said, reaching his hand to her. "I'm putting you to bed."

He removed her shoes, some of her clothes. He lay down beside her and wrapped them both in blankets. He watched as she quivered gently, as if possessed, and he tried to still her with his touch. He listened as she murmured unintelligible sounds back into a struggle he did not understand. And in the thin sliver of time between the night and the morning, he slipped inside of her, and they made love wordlessly, privately, a joining, near joining, not joining, rocking with exhaustion and lonesomeness for each other, and then they separated.

When Sam came home from work the next evening, he saw the signs of Amanda's lying in—an orange juice container stuffed between the pillows of the couch, her untied sneakers at either end, the light summer quilt crumpled on the floor. "Hello?"

She came out of the bathroom still pulling strands of hair out of the ponytail that stood high up on the left side of her head. Sam had often wondered why certain moods of hers required her to do strange things to her hair, but it wasn't something she was ever able to explain and so he had come to accept the asymmetries and the buns gone haywire as temporary sentences. She took a bobby pin out of her mouth and stuck it somewhere in her head. "Hi."

Sam carried the bag of groceries he had been clutching into the kitchen and put them down on the counter. "I figured I'd better pick up a few things."

Amanda nodded and started to unpack them. There were two turkey sandwiches on top and she put them on plates without removing the wax paper. "Mark called a little while ago."

Sam frowned but she didn't see it. "Oh?"

"Yeah. He said he's been waiting to hear from you about a script. What script?"

"Nothing. He just wanted my opinion about some project he's thinking about doing."

"Oh. Is it any good?"

"I haven't had a chance to read it."

"Why didn't you tell me about it?"

"I didn't think of it. It's no big deal, okay?"

"Sure."

She carried the plates to the table and Sam followed behind her with a beer. Even from a few feet away, the smell of it made her convulse.

They sat down across from each other and began to peel the paper off of their sandwiches. Sam started to eat while Amanda picked up the top piece of rye bread and laid it back down a few times.

"I'm sorry about last night," she said, fingering the tomato slice so that the seeds dripped onto the plate.

Sam put down his sandwich and his eyes widened to that kid-at-a-carnival look he had. "Jeez," he said. "Last night was one of the worst nights of my life."

Amanda frowned. "Oh c'mon," she said flatly. "It wasn't that bad."

"Not that bad? I spend half the night waiting for you and then you come in shaking like a wet dog and I don't even know what happened."

"All I can say is if that was one of the worst nights of your life you're doing pretty damn well."

They were someplace else, above or below, they were not where either of them meant to be, back then, start back, start.

"What happened?" Sam asked.

"Nothing happened. I don't know."

"Oh. Well it must have been something. Can you at least try to give me some idea?"

"I'm sorry I don't have a typed up list of answers for you." Not here, back then, start back, start. "Sorry." She pushed her plate away and looked at him, not ready to start. "Besides, I wasn't such a mess that you didn't want to make love to me. If that's what you want to call it."

Sam said nothing, made a little hole in his lip with his front tooth. He pushed his plate away too.

Start someplace else, start here. "I don't know what it

was.'' Her lips were dry and she licked them and her throat was an endless field of lumps. ''I just got lost. It happens.''

''Lost?''

''You know, like I was falling between the spaces. Suddenly I just didn't seem to know where I was, where I was supposed to be.''

''What spaces?''

''Spaces, just spaces. I guess the spaces between what I used to want and what I want now, or the spaces between how I used to be and how I am now and how you think I am and I wasn't any one of those but I was falling in between. You see?''

''Kind of. Maybe. How did you used to be?''

She shrugged. ''See, this bar I was in last night. Well, I used to feel at home there. No, not at home. But I used to take it for granted that I'd never feel at home anywhere so it was okay to be there and then all of a sudden it wasn't okay. It didn't feel okay at all.''

''What made it not okay?''

She smiled. ''You.''

Sam smiled too but he was still confused. ''The thing I don't get is, why didn't you just come home?''

''Don't you ever get lost, Sam?''

''Yes. Yes, of course I do.''

''So?''

It was his turn to shrug.

''Oh Christ,'' Amanda blurted out. ''I just got so scared.''

Sam slid off of his seat and kneeled before her, brushing aside a few loose strands of hair. ''Scared of what?'' Maybe this time.

When she looked down at him it was sad and self-deprecating and he only wanted to hold her. ''I've never been in love before.'' She spit it out like an accusation. ''I know that sounds crazy, but it's true.''

He smiled. ''Neither have I.''

"Really?"

"Really."

"What a pair."

"What a pair."

"So," she said, smiling now, "what do we do?"

"I told you what I think we should do. I think we should get married."

"Really? I mean is that what you really, really want?"

"That's what I really, really want."

"Well," she said, "I guess we might as well."

"Try to contain your enthusiasm."

"You're on your knees," she said. "Go ahead. Propose to me."

Sam smiled and put his hand on his heart. "You are the light of my life, the apple of my eye, you are the sun and the moon and the stars . . ."

Amanda yawned. "That's what they all say."

He rolled his eyes as far as they would go, to the heavens. "Will you marry me?"

"Yes."

"Yes?"

She slid off of her chair, slid to the floor, to him. "Yes."

He sat up tapping his fingers softly on the mattress, not quite meaning to wake her, and yet . . . It was a personal rebuff to him this morning, the way she lay motionless beneath the thin quilt, swaddled in a drowsy half-sleep, unable—or was it unwilling?—to rise, to talk, to give herself up to the day, to him. This day particularly he had awakened sharply, eagerly, filled with a burgeoning desire to get going, to make plans, to make themselves known.

When his impatience could no longer be contained but seemed to bubble up like so much lava, he reached down and shook Amanda's shoulder. "Wake up," he said, his voice pressing, excited.

Amanda shuddered slightly and groaned.

"C'mon. Get up."

"What is this, Christmas?"

"Who should we call first?" Sam asked as he pointed Amanda's head in the direction of the coffee he had already made for her.

She slid her arm out and grabbed it, her face hidden from him by a static halo of hair. She took a few greedy sips and then rested the cup on the pillow, creating a wet brown ring. "Can't it wait?" she asked, still avoiding his eyes.

"No," he answered firmly. "No, it cannot wait."

She took a few more sips of coffee and they both listened to it slide down her throat. Then she put the mug on the floor and slid her hand slowly down his hard chest and stomach until it came almost to his crotch. Sam lifted her arm and put it by her side.

"No," he said.

"No?" Her gray eyes had gone big and opaque.

"No," he smiled. "And don't give me that pitiful look."

Amanda frowned. "Can I ask you something?"

"What?"

"Why is it so important that we rush to tell everyone?"

Sam reset his feet on the ground and stared at her shoulder as it disappeared into the sheets. "Don't you think it's natural to want to share this kind of news?" he asked.

"I suppose."

"But?"

"I just thought maybe we could keep it to ourselves for a little while. I don't know." She squirmed about the bed. "It seems so, you know, private. It's embarrassing to call people up and . . ."

"You mean you're embarrassed to be marrying me?"

"No, of course not." She reached her hand from its hiding place beneath the pillow and put it on his. I am getting married, I want to get married, I want. She shook her head involuntarily. "It's not exactly embarrassment, it's . . ."

"Well thank God for small favors," Sam interrupted.

She shrugged, pulled herself up, kissed his shoulder. "You sure you don't want to fool around a little first?"

"We've been fooling around long enough."

Amanda rolled her eyes. "Don't go getting metaphorical on me. That wasn't part of the deal."

Sam laughed and ran his fingers in circles around her breast. "There's lots of time for that. All the time in the world."

"All the time in the world?"

"Yes. But business first."

"What makes you so sure? I mean about all the time

in the world? This could be it, this morning, this could be all we have . . ."

"C'mon, Chicken Little," Sam said as he pulled her out of bed. "I'm not in the mood for your gloomy meanderings." He pushed her down the hall and sat her on the couch in the living room. The old lace slip she was wearing had slid half off and she covered herself up.

"Sam?"

"What?"

"Is that what you think? That I'm just full of gloomy meanderings?"

"No. But I think it's time for you to stop looking for places to hide."

The stenciled letters of the University logo on his T-shirt were peeling off in sticky white flakes and she became momentarily absorbed in removing part of the v. "Oh."

Sam leaned over and kissed her gently. "I love you."

"I know." She shrugged, she had to let it go. "Okay, you first."

Sam nodded and Amanda watched as he dialed his parents' number in Ohio.

Her toes curled around the hard edge of the toilet seat as she balanced her mug of coffee on her knees and watched Sam shave. At times, it was almost like nausea, this sudden and unexpected wave that would swell from some secret place within and wash over her in an instant—happiness? She wondered if it showed—in a flush, a twinge—it was so alien and intimate to her that it shook her usual sense of balance and left her nervous and unsteady. Sam's torso rose firm and smooth from the pale blue towel wrapped about his waist as he leaned over the sink and regarded himself carefully in the mirror.

"Are you waiting for me to finish?" he asked as he held his head back to reach beneath his chin. It was the second morning that she had sat like this, watching the slow, repetitive motions, keeping him company.

"No. I just like sitting here."

Sam smiled and a puff of lather fell from his face.

"It's probably hopelessly Freudian," Amanda continued. "I used to love watching my father shave. It was our special time together. On good mornings, at least."

She spoke softly, it was a small room, their bodies large and close. Sam stood as still as he could and waited for her to go on but she didn't. He rinsed the remaining lather from his face and reached for a towel to pat himself dry. When he turned around, he was clean and new and she again felt unsteady as she watched him smile and sit down on the floor opposite her.

Amanda laughed in surprise. "What are you doing?"

"I don't know. I thought maybe you'd let me watch you put on your makeup."

"Sam."

"I used to love watching my mother put on her makeup. It was our special time together."

Amanda frowned. "You're making fun of me."

He reached over and pulled on her big toe. "No," he said gently. "No, really I'm not." He smiled apologetically. "We're still making mistakes," he noted quietly, as if to himself. "You know I wish you'd tell me more about your family; what it was like."

"There's nothing to tell."

Sam laughed. "C'mon. Tell me one thing about your father."

"What?"

"Anything. Anything I don't know. That should give you an open enough field."

Amanda thought for a minute. "Okay. When I was a teenager and boys would call, if he answered the phone he would say, 'Why on earth would you want to talk to my daughter? You must be crazy. No one wants to talk to her. You don't want to see her too, do you? My God.' He was only teasing them but he'd go on and on and they would never call back."

"How did you get dates?"

"I learned how to sneak around."

He rubbed her ankle, took it in his hands, saw her as a teenager, sliding sideways past her father. "It must have hurt," he said.

Amanda shrugged. "Not really. It was just the way it was. Let's forget about this twenty questions routine, okay?"

Sam smiled. "Don't you trust me yet?"

"It's not a matter of trust. Look, you don't tell me everything either."

Sam was silent.

"Maybe," Amanda said hesitantly, "maybe we'll always be slightly like strangers to each other."

He considered this. "Maybe."

She smiled and ran her hands through his hair, she was lighter and flirtatious now. "At least it'll keep it interesting."

"Keeping it interesting is not what I'm worried about," Sam answered grimly.

"Oh? What are you worried about?"

He paused, rolled it about like a dark marble, but when he looked at her, it was the public, the gracious way he chose to give her. "Nothing," he said, smiling. "I love you."

"I love you too."

The ringing phone interrupted their kiss. "I'll get it," Amanda said, standing up. "You're already late for work." She went into the living room and picked up the receiver. "Hello?"

"Hello, dear," Mrs. Easton answered.

"Oh. Hi, Mom."

"Well, I know that you must be busy," Mrs. Easton continued as if she were peering through her reading glasses at a prepared text. "So I won't hold you. Just a quick question."

"Yes?"

"What does Sam's father do?"

"Why the hell do you suddenly need to know that?"

"Well, I suppose we should put an engagement announcement in the *Times*."

"Absolutely not, Mother."

Mrs. Easton did not protest but relinquished what she had little enthusiasm for to begin with. She had long ago accepted certain rules of conduct and following them had been as second nature to her. But they were not truly important and whatever energy she could muster was better spent on other matters. "Whatever you want, dear," she said now, without resentment, without relief.

Amanda said good-bye and went into the bedroom to dress, muttering to herself. "The *Times*, Christ."

"Who was it?" Sam asked as he passed her on his way to the door.

"My mother. You're not going to believe what she wanted. She wanted to put an engagement announcement in the *Times*. Can you believe it?"

The rituals of New York society were still unfamiliar to Sam and he wouldn't have cared much one way or the other. What jabbed him was the vehemence in Amanda's voice. "What are you making such a fuss about? Just tell her no if that's what you want."

"I did," Amanda retorted angrily.

"So?"

"Just the thought of it annoys me. I mean, can you see me in a white dress and pearls? Christ. Listing all of the colleges I dropped out of would take two columns alone."

"Look," Sam said. "I'm really late. We'll talk about it tonight."

"There's nothing to talk about."

"Right. Bye." He touched her shoulder and left.

Amanda was rifling through the closet when Sam stuck his head back in the room. "Just how many colleges did you drop out of?" he asked, sort of smiling.

She started to laugh. "Go. You're late."

Amanda threw clothes away. Often, when she was bored or anxious or dissatisfied, she would run her hands through her closets, her drawers, looking for things to discard, as if the culprit of her dissatisfaction lay folded in a pile, hanging from a piece of wire. At times, of course, there were genuine mistakes to be gotten rid of, a blouse bought too hastily that drooped in the shoulders, a demure dress chosen as if for someone else's life, but lately, there had been fewer of those and she was left to incinerate perfectly wearable items. She never gave them away to friends, to charity, never placed them by the door to be reconsidered in a calmer moment—she thrust them down the chute immediately and then rushed back inside to see if there was anything else she could rid herself of. "The disappeared," Sam called them.

In fact, her seemingly total lack of nostalgia shocked him anew each time he saw evidence of it. For it was not just clothes that she incinerated, but letters, odds and ends that others would consider mementos, even memories themselves, for with the exception of her occasional pointillist offerings, she claimed to remember only the barest particulars of her childhood. He suspected that her habit of shaking her head sharply at odd times and for no apparent reason was her attempt to dislodge any disquieting thought from her mind. Sometimes, he wondered if she would turn to his things next, sneaking a shirt, a book, a photograph away from him when he wasn't looking, systematically erasing all but the present.

Now she stood before the old-fashioned oval mirror that rested in the front room of Legacies, holding a new dress pressed to her body as she examined her own reflection. Sometimes she spent hours, draping herself in scarves, painting an exotic face on top of her own, colored with crimsons or pastels, looking for an armament, looking for a clue. In stores, she would reach for disparate answers, a long flowery dress, a leather miniskirt, is this it? or is it this? For she knew that she could—when it was working, when it was right—mold her attitude to the chosen garment like an actress to a role, and surely there must be some comfort in that. She tugged the bodice up higher. The dress was made of a thin black silk that was cold and slippery to the touch, cut on the bias like a slip, with delicate straps and a scalloped border across the chest. She freed one hand and pulled back her hair. She would have a whitened matte face, dark red lips, a perfect martini before her . . .

"So have you told Sally yet?" Nancy asked as she glanced up from the lengthy purchase orders rustled across the counter.

"No."

"Why not?"

"Because she'll get that 'I told you so' look in her eyes that makes me want to strangle her." Amanda put the dress on a velvet quilted hanger.

Nancy laughed. "You make it sound like you're admitting defeat, not getting married."

Amanda began to unpack various sizes of the slip dress and hang them side by side. It only came in black. "I'll call her later," she said.

Nancy sat down on the low yellow footstool that she had picked up at a thrift shop a few weeks ago. "You sounded so happy when you told me the other day."

"I am happy. I just don't see why people have to make such a big deal about it."

"Getting married is a big deal."

Amanda had run out of dresses to hang up. She went back to the size eights and made sure that their straps were straight.

"Amanda," Nancy said almost warily. "It's natural to be apprehensive."

"I know. It's just . . ." she turned from the rack and looked at Nancy. "You know what I spent half of last night thinking about?"

"What?"

"All the things that I would never do. I mean, I suddenly can't just pick up and run off to the south of France, I can't lust after dark-eyed strangers . . ."

Nancy laughed.

Amanda hardly smiled before she continued. "It was like looking down a long corridor and seeing one door after another shut in my face."

"But chances are you wouldn't do those things anyway."

"I know that. That's not the point. It's the idea of saying, This is it, that terrifies me. It seems so final."

"But it's not final. It's just deciding to take a different approach, to do it with someone."

"I know. I mean, that's how I feel. Most of the time. And I love him. I really do love him. It's the closest I've ever come to feeling safe."

"Catch-22?"

"Exactly."

"So?"

She was looking at her feet now, at the rug, she didn't know what it was. "I don't know how to explain this to you," she said. "I'm not even sure I understand it myself. I mean, I know I don't. I tried talking about it to Bill once, but . . . anyway, a long time ago, I know this sounds sick, but I used to sit in closets. This one closet I had. Not all the time, but when things were bad, when they were closing in, I would just climb into this closet and shut the door and crawl behind the clothes and I'd stay there for hours and hours. The thing is, I knew the

91

whole time I was in there that it wasn't normal, wasn't right, that I shouldn't spend whole afternoons sitting in a closet, but there was also this little voice saying I could get out anytime, and that made it sort of okay, because I knew what I was doing, like I was watching myself, seeing how far I was willing to go with it. And that's what made it so terrifying, so confusing. Because I never could figure out if I was crazy because I was sitting in this closet for hours or not crazy because I knew I was doing it or even crazier because I was watching it and I'd just go round and round with it." Amanda shifted her weight, looked up, smiled. "You know what Bill said?"

"What?"

"He said it didn't make a hell of a bit of difference what I was aware of, what I was watching, all that mattered was the fact, and the fact was I was sitting in a closet."

"Would you mind telling me what all this has to do with getting married?"

Amanda shrugged. "I don't know. Nothing, I guess." She began to laugh. "I bet if I tried to tell Sam about it he'd want to know how many shirts were in the closet."

"That's not true."

"No, it's not true. But you see, what bothers me is that I can't believe that Bill was right. I mean, is it just a matter of changing facts? Doesn't the rest make a difference?"

"I don't know."

"Oh well," Amanda sighed and lightened up from behind. "My closet days are long since gone, right? I am now the picture of maturity, stability and sense. And besides, I'm no spring chicken. Who knows, this could be my one big chance at domestic bliss."

"Right."

"Nancy? Forget about all this, okay? It's stupid. I'm happy. I really am. Maybe that's what it is, who knows.

Maybe I'm so fucking happy it terrifies me. Everything always disintegrated before."

Nancy stood up, smiling. "I know what we should do. I'm going to throw you a party." The idea began to unfold in her mind and she was propelled across the room by it. "A big engagement party is just the ticket. The kind where everyone drinks too much and flirts with all the wrong people and only pretends to regret it in the morning." She grabbed a fresh pad, picked up her pen.

Amanda laughed. "Is your strategy to remind me of all I won't be missing?"

"The strategy, my dear, is fun." She rapidly began to make up a list of names.

Amanda watched for a second, shrugged, and then went to lean over the pad. "What the hell," she said, "let's do it. But just remember, this was your idea." And she began to add to the growing lineup as they both went through their books, stopping now and then to comment on one or another's dreadful new haircut, questionable proclivities, impending separation.

Just as they were finishing, Deirdre walked into the store, fifteen minutes late, cheerful and unconcerned—they obviously hadn't had any customers yet. "Morning, girls." Her glittering brightness, her clear blue twenty-one-year-old eyes and her platinum hair and her incessantly playful manner had lately begun to make Amanda feel leaden, dull and oafish and moribund.

"You two have got to check out that new club uptown," she said as she dropped her shiny yellow bag behind the register. "It's got a waterfall in the middle of the dance floor and this really cool guy bought me champagne all night and . . ."

Amanda looked at Nancy and groaned. "Was I ever that young?" she asked.

"No," Nancy said. "I don't think you ever were."

Deirdre looked from one to the other and then she began to laugh.

"**W**hy didn't you tell me when you wrote?" she asked. "Why did I have to hear about it from your mother?"

Sam played with the papers on his desk. "I didn't know about it when I wrote." She was gone to him, already stored away with the rest of the dead, the embalmed, the unnecessary, he hadn't planned on her at all.

"Well," Cathy went on, "I think you at least owe me some sort of an explanation."

"I wrote you that I was staying here."

"You wrote me a lot of things. You're very good at that. You want to know what I hated most about that letter?"

He continued doodling on the side of a page proof. It used to be enough for him to smile at Cathy, to burrow beneath the field between them, assured that she would not attempt to cross it, that she did not even see it. It had been his comfort, it had been his grace, his freedom, that unacknowledged space between them; it had been one of the holding points. "What?"

"The part about me misinterpreting things. How dare you? You can't just dismiss all the years we spent together like that. You don't have that right."

"I'm sorry."

She took a deep breath and he could hear it, feel its in out, he knew how she looked with her deep green eyes and her perfect bob, he knew how she felt in his hands, small, curved, he used to be able to predict what she would say almost all the time so that he had been able to look away, go someplace else, only alight when he felt like it, sure that she would be just where he had left her, she let out her breath now. "Sam," she said quietly, "I still love you. And I want you to be happy. I can't help it, I think we belong together. I always have. I thought you did too."

And that knowing was like a thicket of strings, for she was too familiar to dismiss, too familiar to love. "We want different things, Cathy," he said.

"How do you know what I want?"

"Okay. I want different things."

"What things? How do you know I can't give them to you if you won't tell me what they are? That's not fair. You can't just make these big decisions and not even give me a chance."

"They're not things one person can ask for, get from another. It's not that simple."

"If it's not that simple, why are you marrying someone else?"

"I told you, we both agreed, it was over between us. A long time ago. You knew that."

Her anger receded for a moment. "I guess I didn't think you'd stay away. I can't imagine you anyplace else, not really, not for good. I always thought you'd come back."

"I don't belong there. Not anymore."

"And you belong in New York?"

"I might."

"That doesn't sound very convincing."

"I belong here."

"You have it all worked out then?" The sardonic tone was new.

"Of course not. But at least I'm trying."

"I see. Well then I guess we have nothing left to say to each other."

"Wait." Suddenly, it was too abrupt. Like one who

95

must wait impatiently for a fire to go out before retiring but cannot resist poking the embers and watching them glow, he tried to pull her back. "Wait. I mean, we're still friends, aren't we? At least tell me what's been going on in your life."

Cathy laughed and it hurt enough for two. "Oh please. You've got to be kidding." She slammed down the phone.

Sam sat motionless for a minute before he hung up the receiver. For as long as he could remember, there had been this constant, this smooth and predictable and safe haven, to resent, to rebel against, to return to, Cathy.

He pushed the phone a couple of inches away and returned to the pages before him, a bevy of new French and German films critiqued by guest celebrities. He moved the sentences, the paragraphs, up and down, juxtaposing them with rather nasty drawings of stars from both sides of the Atlantic. There was no constant now, no haven—there was only Amanda.

The photos lined the deep royal blue walls of the entranceway, the lights from above bouncing and disseminating off of the glass frames so that the viewers had to tilt their heads sideways, stoop just slightly, to see the prints—blowups of tenement kitchens, exaggerated details of peeling paint, beer cans in commodes, tattooed boys posing with sneers of carefully rehearsed rebellion glued onto their gaunt faces.

Sam had been there since noon, walking in circles about the echoing dance floor as workers poured ammonia on top of last night's spilled liquor and ashes. When he had first arrived, most of the pictures were stacked haphazardly in a corner, as if someone had suddenly run out of nails, or interest, and there was a message for him that the band he had hired had had their equipment stolen. Sam's eyes glazed—it was the first big event he was responsible for. The club owner, a small balding man in a navy Brooks Brothers suit and a Yankees cap, found his panic amusing. "Chill out," he said calmly. "It'll pull together somehow. It always does, doesn't it?" And then he turned his attention back to a disgruntled liquor salesman.

Sam found a hammer and some nails and began to mount the exhibit himself. He worked quickly, remembering as he glanced at his watch every couple of minutes how he used to set it fifteen minutes behind when he had first moved to New York, embarrassed by his hopeless punctuality, his unavoidable sense of propriety. Now, as he gradually began to see the neat lineup of frames take shape, he began to relax.

At four-thirty, Sam stepped out of the semicircle of colleagues and friends that surrounded him and surveyed the room. The band had managed to borrow the proper equipment, the pictures were evenly hung, and people had come, despite his reservations about the party being held in the afternoon. "Don't they have jobs?" he had asked Patrick when the plans were first being formulated. "They'll come," Patrick assured him. "It will be a novelty. And cheaper for us." He looked up from the cuffs of his shirt. "Don't be so middle-class," he chided.

Sam felt something brush up against his ear and as he turned around his head collided with Lucy, a *Backlog* photographer and author of the book. They both laughed as they touched their damaged foreheads. She reached over and kissed him. "Thanks," she whispered. She had thick black hair that fell in waves and ringlets to her waist and amber skin that promised all the warmth of the Mediterranean.

Sam smiled. "For what?"

"That's what I like, modesty in a man. This does have something to do with you, doesn't it?"

In fact, Sam didn't think it had anything to do with him. At least he hoped not. "No problem," he said.

Lucy continued to smile at him. They were exactly the same height and she held his eyes with hers, dark and confident and luminous. "Why don't we have dinner later?" she asked.

"I can't. I mean, well look, my girlfriend, I mean my fiancée . . ."

She laughed in an easy, relaxed manner that made Sam feel even more foolish. "I didn't mean to make you so nervous," she said.

Sam took a breath and smiled. "I'm not nervous. I just didn't want you to think, I mean, normally, I'd love to . . ."

"But these are abnormal times?"

Sam laughed. "These are abnormal times."

Lucy reached into her large ostrich bag and pulled out a small black card with her name and number embossed in silver. Smiling still, she reached inside of Sam's jacket and put the card in his pocket. "In case you change your mind." Sam watched as she walked slowly away, her red dress draping her perfect ass.

"I'll take that," Mark said, coming up behind him and pretending to reach for the card.

Sam laughed. "Not so fast."

"I thought I heard you were getting married."

"I am. Why aren't you sitting by the pool of the Beverly Hills Hotel hustling up a deal?"

"I'm waiting for you."

"I'm sorry, Mark. I've been so busy lately, I haven't had a chance to think about it."

"I always said you could give Hamlet a run for his money. Seriously, I do need an answer. How about next week?"

"Could we, I mean, if I decided to do it, could we do it nights and weekends?"

"No, I told you, they want the script pretty quickly. It's worth the gamble, Sam."

"I'm not a gambling man. I'm more the bird-in-hand type."

"Even if what you have in your hand is bird shit?"

"I'm glad you think so highly of my career."

"That's not what I mean, you know that. I also know that you'd be much better off hitching a ride with me."

"Maybe. And maybe I'd end up flat broke with no job."

Mark smiled. "You know what they say, 'Life is a risk, only death is certain.' "

"With lines like that, you do need a writer."

"So?"

"So, I think I'd better go circulate. I'll talk to you later, okay?"

"Okay."

Sam walked quickly away. He had read the treatment, three times, read it and thought about it and fantasized what he would do if he could do it but of course he couldn't, how could he? No, he couldn't. You just don't do things like that. No. Of course not. He shook his head and went up to say hello to the West Coast sales director.

Amanda arrived twenty minutes later. Sam looked busy so she went over to the bar and got herself a spritzer, stopping to chat a bit with the bartender, who she had spent a few evenings with years ago. When he had too many backed-up drink orders to keep reminiscing, she turned around and faced the party, spotting Sam once more at the other end of the room, smiling as he walked from circle to circle, the perfect host of a party of strangers. He moved with an automatic hard confidence, like a figure skater barely cutting the ice, and she watched curiously, looking for scratch marks. Finally, she walked over to him.

"How's it going?" she asked as she kissed him hello.

"Great." He was still smiling that hard smooth smile but there was a sharp corner in his voice that made her step back and look at him questioningly.

"Well I for one am having a good time," she said cheerfully, and he knew that it was probably true.

They stayed and mingled through the band's second set and then they began to make their rounds of goodbyes, just as other people were gradually doing the same. As they headed for the clotted exit, Sam turned around and saw Lucy seated at a table with some friends, laughing as she dipped a cookie in her wine and ate it. The card was like a coal in his pocket.

Out on the street, Sam put his arm around Amanda's waist, wondering if she would ever feel like his.

M aggie moved restlessly within Amanda's loose circular grasp, the bright pink of her corduroy overalls rubbing against the worn Oriental rug where they sat together on the floor. A few feet away, Sally was perched on her bicycle machine, the shiny nylon suit she was wearing squeaking in rhythm with her rapid pedaling. Her hair was pulled up with a polka dot ribbon into a pony-tail at the exact top of her head, and underneath, it was closer to Amanda's light brown than the lightened ends that were pointing to the ceiling.

"And Maggie can be the flower girl," she panted. "Would you like that, sweetie pie?"

Amanda frowned. "Sam and I want a really simple wedding. Just the immediate family. Maybe in Mom's apartment."

"And does the bride plan on wearing black?"

"Maybe. Look Sally, we're just not into all that hoopla. I'd feel like a jerk carrying a bunch of flowers."

"I felt like a lot of things walking down the aisle. But I did not feel like a jerk." Sally wiped her forehead with the back of her hand, but it was still cool and dry. "That took years," she said. "So, have you set a date?"

"No. But as soon as possible. We might as well get it over with."

"You make it sound like surgery."

"Well it does feel a little life-threatening at times."

Sally stopped pedaling and leaned back against the wall, propping her puffy white Reeboks on the handlebars.

"Amanda, this is the worst part. The arrangements and all. Once that's over with, you'll be fine."

Amanda recognized her sister's attempts at reassurance and smiled absently at Maggie. "I know. I want to be his wife. I just don't want to get married," she said, laughing at herself.

"Why can't you look on it as fun?"

She rearranged her legs beneath her. "I don't know. Maybe I'm superstitious. It's been my experience that as soon as you make too many plans for something, it's certain to fall apart."

"That's ridiculous."

"Okay. It'll be fun," she said. "In the meantime," she held up her watch for Sally to see, "it hasn't been twenty minutes."

"Frank'll never know." She climbed off of the machine and walked over to Maggie, picked her up, kissed her, put her down. "Why don't you go make a drawing for Amanda," she said as she headed her in the direction of her room. She turned back to Amanda and loosened her ponytail. "You should see the chart he made up for me last weekend. His latest theory is that my problems are caused by," she began to imitate Frank's humorless manner, "my inability to properly utilize my time."

"Christ," Amanda moaned. And then asked, "What problems?"

Sally smiled. "Problems? Did I say problems?" She unzipped her top and slipped on a striped cotton sweater. "C'mon, let's go plan your betrothal."

"Speaking of problems . . ."

"That's not what I meant."

They sat at the black marble dining room table sipping at large glasses of Sancerre that Sally had poured for them.

"Are Sam's parents flying in?"

"I guess so."

"Aren't you dying to meet them?"

"I don't think they're dying to meet me. They wanted him to marry that other girl."

"The hometown hussy?"

Amanda laughed. "Besides, what if Dad goes haywire? They don't sound like the kind of people who'd understand that sort of thing."

"What's the matter, don't you think they have drunken assholes in Ohio too?"

Amanda frowned.

"Sorry," Sally said begrudgingly.

"Look, I'm sure it will all work out. Why don't we just talk about something else for a change?"

"Fine. What would you like to discuss? Nicaragua? The new wing at the Met? I know. I forgot to tell you about this job interview I went on the other day. This guy just out of college sat me down in front of a colored graph and asked me to rate my personality. It was phenomenal. All these purple and red and blue bars for leadership ability, honesty, ambition. Can you imagine putting up with that kind of nonsense?" Sally finished her wine and poured herself another full glass. "You know what Frank said when I told him about it? He said it sounded innovative. Innovative," she said, shaking her head and smiling. "I thought it sounded like an experiment in bullshit."

"What was the job?"

"Who cares?"

"I'll tell you, I wish Sam would find himself a different job."

"Why? What's wrong with *Backlog*? I thought he just got that big promotion?"

"He did, but it's still not the right place for him."

"So why doesn't he leave?"

"I don't know exactly. Everytime I bring it up, he gets so defensive that I've stopped trying. He has this thing about a weekly paycheck that no one's going to talk him out of. I think he forgot that *Backlog* was only supposed to be a temporary measure until he could do what he really wanted."

"What does he really want to do?"

Amanda smiled. "To tell you the truth, I don't know. I don't even think he does. Something different. Something more."

"Well maybe you'll balance each other out. You average five different jobs a year and he Krazy Glues himself into one he can't stand."

Amanda laughed. "That's not fair. In case you haven't noticed, I've been at Legacies for over a year now. Remember, I'm a partner. You happen to be looking at responsible management."

"Oh God," Sally groaned, "a born-again career girl. Spare me."

They were both laughing when Maggie came waddling into the room and stood before Amanda, her chubby face grave and anxious. With great ceremony she placed a piece of yellow construction paper on her aunt's lap and waited, watching as she held it up to admire.

"It's beautiful," Amanda said. "Thank you." She hadn't the vaguest idea of what it was supposed to be.

Sally leaned over and looked at the drawing. "What a pretty sailboat," she gushed, and pulled her daughter onto her lap.

Amanda watched as mother and daughter snuggled so contentedly together, marveling as always at their secret language that she could not begin to understand.

Across the ceiling pipes of their loft, Nancy had hung a long line of paper lanterns with bulbs of different colors within that made them glow like globs of pastel cotton candy. The large mission table that had been her grandmother's was covered with food in various states of picked-over disarray and the rising din indicated that the party was just hitting its stride.

"You look great tonight," Jack said to Amanda as he refilled her glass.

"Careful," Sam warned. "She doesn't take compliments well."

Amanda turned to him, smiling. "How would you know? When was the last time you tried?"

"Now children," Jack scolded.

Sam tugged gently at the narrow strap of Amanda's black slip of a dress and wandered away to greet a friend.

"So," Jack said as he stepped a little closer. "We've been thinking about what to get you as a wedding present."

"And?"

"I'm in favor of a year's free legal assistance, just in case. By me, of course."

"Very funny."

"A marriage contract?"

"Unfortunately, worldly wealth doesn't play a big part in this."

"Well, you could use it to make Sam swear to take the garbage out every Tuesday and make love to you the second Thursday of every month."

"Is that what makes your marriage so successful?"

As if on cue, Nancy joined the conversation. "Are you giving away all of our secrets, darling?"

"You know us lawyers, we're full of leaks."

"Full of something, anyway," Amanda said.

Jack reached over and playfully mussed her hair. She had made her face pale, her lips dark red.

"C'mon," Nancy said, pulling her away. "You have a social obligation to mingle."

The loft was a collage now, filled with traces of different lives, family, friends, business acquaintances, touching, overlapping, colliding—the very thing that Amanda had always avoided, as if she feared that they would compare notes, discover—what? She had jumped from piece to piece at first, not stopping long enough to mar the party gloss, not stopping long enough to be caught. But she began to relax as she and Nancy approached the open kitchen and found Deirdre in the corner by the stove, surrounded by three men.

"The Scarlett O'Hara of Soho," Amanda remarked.

"Does she remind you of your own misspent youth?"

"I beg your pardon."

"Seriously," Nancy said quietly as she leaned up against Amanda's ear, "do you think we should talk to her about safe sex?"

"A contradiction in terms if ever there was one."

"I mean it. I feel responsible for her."

"Look," Amanda said, "she's probably a lot better off than we are. Don't forget, she came of age during this nightmare. She probably knows more uses for a condom than you can shake a mascara wand at."

Nancy laughed uneasily and went to replenish the crudités.

Amanda wandered down the long hallway past the closed door to the nursery and into the large front area where people had begun to dance to an early James Brown tape. She could tell by her novocaine legs that she had drunk a little too quickly and she was glad of it, glad to rest in the distance and defiance it gave her.

"So," Bill said, coming up behind her, "tell me. What circle do you think this is?" He was imitating her voice played at the wrong speed and smiling with a tolerance and complicity they had found in foxholes long ago.

Amanda laughed. "Okay, okay. So I had one bad night." She kissed him on the lips. "It was just a temporary setback."

Bill smiled and looked about the room. "And this is what you really want?"

"This is what I really want."

"I still think it's just a phase, one of your fly-by-night whims that somehow made it to the morning."

"Fuck you, Bill."

He smiled and she smiled too, she had to.

"Why can't you accept this side of me?" she asked.

"Because I've never seen it before. I've known you an awfully long time, Amanda, and this is new to me."

"Maybe you just didn't want to see it."

"If I didn't, neither did you."

"Are you so sure it's a matter of sides?"

Bill smiled. "You should know by now, I'm not sure of anything."

Amanda leaned over and kissed him. "Neither am I. But let's just fake it, okay?"

"I've told you before, you never get what you want if you fake it."

Amanda frowned. "Do me a favor, Bill. Go find yourself someone else to dance with. I'm going to go over and find out what Mark and Sam have been so tied up with." She kissed him once more and pushed him playfully away from her.

"You two look like back-room politicians," she said as she came up behind them and wrapped her arm about Sam's neck. "What are you plotting?"

"It doesn't look like we'll be plotting much of any-thing," Mark answered.

"Huh?"

"Nothing," Sam said.

Amanda looked at them both and shrugged. "C'mon," she began to pull Sam away, "let's dance."

"That was a little rude," Sam said as he held her in his arms for a ballad.

"Well I think it's rude for you to shut up the minute I come near."

Sam said nothing but Amanda could feel his back stiffen slightly and it annoyed her. She pulled him in tighter and whispered, "You know what I'd like to do?"

There was a note of daring in her voice that both tempted and repelled him. "What?" he asked flatly.

"I'd like to fuck our brains out."

"Later," he said, laughing a little nervously.

"No, now. Right here on the dance floor."

"What have you been drinking?"

"Love potion number nine." She was laughing, but he wasn't sure at what, at who.

When the song ended, Sam released her. "Look, I should go back and talk to Mark," he said. "I was trying to explain something to him."

"Fine."

They spent the next couple of hours lost in different pockets of friends and flirtations, only occasionally inter-secting. It was almost three in the morning when they finally got into a cab, both tired and sober—for Amanda had stopped drinking after her dance with Sam, chas-tened, sorry, scared of running into trouble. Sam leaned his head against the window. "Do you really feel I don't compliment you?" he asked, as if that was what they had been discussing without a break since early in the evening.

"Well, you've never once even told me you like the way I look."

"That's not true."

"Okay."

"Everytime I try," Sam continued, "you say something sarcastic."

"I can't remember you ever trying," Amanda insisted.

They rode through a series of green lights in silence.

"I do like the way you look," Sam said as he got out his wallet. "Very much."

Amanda smiled. "Thank you. I like the way you look very much too."

Sam paid the driver and they climbed out.

B elow her, his face was dusky against the white pillow, his eyes shining up and his lips curling just slightly, in a smile, his granite face of planes and shadows, sure of himself, of her, of the equations of desire . . .

She was propped up on her knees, her elbows, looking down into this face, so sharp she thought she could slice herself on it—she did not want him to smile at her, that's not what she wanted at all, this charming ready smile that fit so easily into the perfect handsome symmetry of his face. At times, it seemed almost willfully masklike, meticulously constructed to keep all blurred edges, all splattering, at bay—even here, even now.

She would crash through it if she could, find whatever it was that would render their manners and their diffidence archaic. For she knew that it was in her too, this translucent barrier that seemed so hopelessly impermeable, their mutual detachment that made them observers of even their own love.

She pinned his hands firmly behind him with swift motions—he was smiling still—and she lowered herself, bit his lip hard—looked to see that his eyes were questioning now, puzzled and excited as he rose to meet her, and she pulled away: No, not yet. His head remained a few inches from the pillow, waiting, and then, just as she began to come closer, he pulled it in like a turtle so that she banged against his hard shell. She bit him again—let me in. She wanted to hurt him now, to hear him cry out. He never really had before, she hadn't either . . .

But when she looked at him again and saw his eyes—baffled, stubborn, kind—she felt suddenly foolish and clumsy, and she softened her grasp and he rolled on top of her. She relented to their usual lovemaking, satisfying and sane.

Sam woke in the middle of the night to find Amanda's side of the bed empty. He waited drowsily for a few minutes—perhaps she was in the bathroom—but when the bed remained empty, he pulled himself up and walked into the living room.

She was silhouetted on the couch, the street lights outlining her pale gown, as she sat hugging her knees to her, her head resting on her arms. He went and sat beside her though he did not try to hold her.

"What is it?" he asked softly.

She was unable to answer him and could only shrug instead. She was shaking slightly, not crying, but quivering as if cold or frightened. He reached his arm around her shoulders.

"Is there anything I can do?" he asked.

She shifted her eyes slowly to his and let out her breath. "Can you hold me so tight it squeezes out the rest of the world?" Her voice was soft and childlike.

Sam smiled a little sadly. "No," he said. "I don't think I can hold you that tight."

Nevertheless, her shaking began to subside. "No, I guess not." She raised her head from her arms and rested it in the hollow of his neck.

"Sam?"

"Yes?"

"Let's get married."

Sam laughed lightly. "I thought we already agreed on that."

"No, I mean now. Let's just do it. I can't stand all this wedding junk and families and people congratulating us like we won a dinette set on a game show. I just can't stand it."

"I know."

"Then let's just go off, by ourselves. Please."

"We can't."

"Why not?"

"Our families, for one thing."

"To hell with our families."

Sam waited.

"Okay, look," Amanda went on. "What about Labor Day weekend? Can't your parents just fly in for that? We can get married in my parents' apartment."

He played with the edges of her gown. "What about a honeymoon?"

"We can do it later. Please, Sam."

There was a note of desperation in her voice that Sam would do anything to quell, to forget. "Okay," he said.

"Promise?"

"Promise. Now come back to bed, okay?"

"In a few minutes. You go on. I just want to sit up for a little while longer."

Amanda watched as Sam stood reluctantly up and began to walk down the hallway. He turned slowly and looked at her for a minute. "I love you," he said quietly.

She smiled. "I love you too. Very much."

Sam climbed back into the disheveled bed and pulled the sheets up to his ear, feeling relieved that some unspecified danger had been sidestepped. For he didn't know what else to do but continue to stand guard over their carefully ordered, often precariously balanced stability, and anything that threatened this, he felt obligated to shut out. But in the moment of shutting it out, he recorded a loss, another loss.

He plumped the pillows, tried moving his legs into a more comfortable position, as he waited for Amanda to return. He knew by now that the stability he created was not the same as serenity, but he hoped that that would follow.

With his hollowed eyes scooped from his face and smudged with dark gray semicircles, and his thick midnight hair that fell across his deeply lined brow, with his rectangular chin held perfectly upright, he was Lord Byron and Frankenstein in one. His mellifluous baritone voice covered the room like a blanket, as if he were playing to a vast audience, though there were fewer than twenty people present, and like a blanket, Sam and Amanda rode across it, all words, all meaning lost to the dramatic tenor of his voice, narcotic and numbing. Sam squeezed Amanda's hand and she returned to the words, ". . . and love is the only thing that never dies . . ."

The rings slipped on their fingers as if by foreign hands, outside, gone, and their mouths were strangers' mouths when they kissed, feeling the first sparks of familiarity only toward the end of the embrace when they dug into each other, mining for solid ground, and everything else slid away, outside, gone, until, almost finding it, they were able to pull apart and embrace.

"Well," Sam whispered in her ear.

"Well," Amanda whispered in his.

The two servants Mrs. Easton had hired for the afternoon popped open the champagne and suddenly there were all those other lips kissing them, all those other arms embracing them.

Amanda found herself engulfed within the great sagging bulk of Mrs. Chapman's arms. "Welcome," Sam's mother said as she kissed her on the cheek. "Welcome,

113

honey." Her voice was unexpectedly guttural, deepened by thirty years of Camels. Amanda had no idea what she was being welcomed to, the Chapman family, a new club—married women, but she smiled and said thank you, leaving behind a wet doughnut on Mrs. Chapman's silk dress where it had gotten caught in her mouth.

Mrs. Chapman continued to touch her, fingering her hair, her forearm, her waist, moving in and in. "I'm sorry you couldn't come to the airport with Sam last night. Of course, we understood, you had so much to do for today. We just want a chance to get to know you, honey. Well, we'll have plenty of time for that tomorrow, won't we?" As she spoke, she reached an arm out to her son and pulled him in too. "Sam, sweetie, are you sure someone's taking pictures? I brought my camera just in case." She opened her white beaded bag and fondled a little Instamatic.

Sam laughed and kissed her softly powdered cheek. "Don't worry, Mom. It's all taken care of." He straightened the orchid that was pinned to her chest. "Did you settle into the hotel okay?"

"Well of course. I love hotels. But I have to tell you, we spent the whole night listening to them dig up the street. Last time I was here, it must be fourteen, fifteen years ago, it was the same thing, them digging all night. I'd stake my life it was the same street too. Putting up, tearing down, putting up, tearing down, just for something to do. This is some city you have here. Isn't anyone ever satisfied?" she asked Amanda.

Mr. Chapman sidled over and patted Sam on the back. "Don't go listening to her. She was out before I could even turn the TV off." He turned to his daughter-in-law. "Sam told us you were pretty. He wasn't lying."

"Thank you."

"Now you two don't mind us. We know you have other people to talk to. We'll just go on over and introduce ourselves around. Schmooze, isn't that what they say?"

Sam laughed. "Where did you get that from, Mom?"

She smiled. "Some movie we rented last week. We keep up on things, you know, even in Ohio."

Mr. Chapman rolled his eyes. "C'mon Pat. I don't know what you call it, but I'm going to shake a few hands."

Sam was still laughing as he watched them walk into the dining room where hors d'oeuvres had been set up. "They'll probably know more about our friends than we do within half an hour."

"Great."

He put his arm around her and kissed her neck. "C'mon. They're getting a kick out of this." His eyes were still on them, like colorful paper dolls, cutouts that had nothing to do with him.

Amanda smiled and nodded. Her own parents were off in separate corners, accepting congratulations of their own.

"Let's go get something to eat," Amanda said and they walked together into the crowded dining room as everyone watched.

Amanda's Aunt Lydia pulled her aside before she could make her way through the women in their pale summer dresses and the men in lightweight suits. "It's been so long," her aunt said. "Our family is just atrocious about getting together, isn't it? Well, this is a lovely day. Of course, I knew it wasn't going to be formal, but . . . well anyway, your mother did a very nice job. You know her, though, she didn't tell me anything about it at all. Now fill me in, darling, how did you two meet?"

"Through a friend."

"Yes, I always think that works best, too. I don't suppose your mother told you about your cousin Matthew, though. He met a simply wonderful young woman in his last semester of law school, and now they're moving to New York. You really should look them up. I'm sure he'd be delighted. Now Christopher, of course . . ."

Amanda nodded and strayed beyond her aunt's dyed head, beyond the family litany, strayed over the chattering guests and the white candles burning in the middle of the table and the disjointed arms reaching for food, to Sam, standing in between Jack and his father and laughing with all the ease of a visiting diplomat. He was wearing a dark suit that she had never seen him in before and he looked handsome and competent and mature. My husband, she thought, but it had no more weight than a schoolgirl's wishful scrawling of a name, my husband, concrete now, but no closer to real, my husband, in the corner, Sam. He caught her eye and smiled and it was a tunnel all their own—we did it.

". . . Now Christopher, of course, has never been happier since he left. You must go visit their new house . . ."

Amanda nodded. Across the room, Nancy wagged her finger at her and she forced herself to look away.

". . . it needs major renovation, but the architect they hired said . . ."

Mary, the Eastons' housekeeper for the past twenty-five years, was moving about on soundless rubber-soled feet with a tray of glistening champagne flutes, and out of the corner of her eye, Amanda saw her father's arm reach out and remove one. She looked quickly back to Sam but he was no longer there.

"Will you excuse me for a minute?" she said to her aunt as she started to walk away, "I have to go talk to my sister about something." She went quickly to the head of the table and took the full plate from Sally's hands and put it down. "Come here," she said, taking her arm. "I need to talk to you." Sally frowned as she let herself be pulled by the elbow from the room.

Amanda didn't say anything until they were safely back in her old bedroom at the end of the hallway, the door locked. They sat down automatically on the floor and leaned their heads against the single bed that still had the white and blue cornflower quilt that she had despised as a teenager.

"What's this all about?" Sally asked.

"Dad."

"What about him?"

"I saw him take a drink. Sally, you've got to help me. If he ruins today, I'll never forgive him."

Sally slid out of her pumps and rubbed her toes for a minute. "Well what am I supposed to do about it?"

"I don't know. I don't care. Anything. Take him to a bar, lock him in the bathroom, throw him out the window, I don't give a damn. Just keep him away from Sam's parents."

She put her shoes back on and grimaced just a little. "Have you warned Sam?"

"Not yet. Anyway, he doesn't know what it's like." Amanda was staring across the room now, lost in the black-and-white checkered psychedelia of the box that used to hold her 45's.

"Okay look," Sally said as she stood up and offered her hand to Amanda, "I'll try to keep an eye on him. But we both know that's a ridiculous notion. Who knows? Maybe this time he'll be okay."

"Just try, Sally."

They unlocked the door and slipped back inside the party.

"Where have you been hiding?" Sam asked as he waylaid her in the living room. "I've been looking for you." He kissed her on the softest spot just behind her ear and his lips were tender and lingering but they hardly touched her.

"Sam, my father's drinking."

"Yeah, I know. But it's only champagne. Why not just let him celebrate? What harm can he do today?"

"You don't understand." He had never seen the alchemy, the immediate possession that once started was impossible to halt, until, by some equally incomprehensible whim, it left him. "Do me a favor, okay? Try to keep your parents away from him."

He smiled. "I've never been able to keep my mother away from anything in my life. Relax. They probably won't even notice. They're much too busy taking pictures of each other." He put his arm protectively about her waist. She was wearing a pale pink and gray antique silk dress that felt smooth and fragile in his hands. "It'll be fine."

Amanda kissed him distractedly and went to talk to Nancy.

"Help," she moaned. "I need some comic relief."

"That's why God invented the wedding night."

An hour later, as Amanda was walking out of the guest bedroom, she came upon Sam, pinned against the wall by her father's long arms, his red-flocked face an inch from Sam's. She froze, mortified, entranced, as she watched Sam smiling nervously into Mr. Easton's intense glare.

He freed one hand from the wall and waved an empty glass menacingly at Sam. "One last thing," he said in a low, fierce voice. "If you ever do anything to hurt her, I'll kill you." The tip of his glass brushed Sam's nose as he nodded politely.

Amanda didn't wait to see how Sam would disentangle himself, but walked quickly into the living room, where her mother and Mrs. Chapman were standing together by the window. "Of course, I suggested she register at Tiffany's," Mrs. Easton was saying as her eyes floated about Mrs. Chapman's fleshy cheeks, "but you know how they are . . ."

"Well Sam did mention that she was a little unconventional."

"I suppose. Well, she can always change her mind."

Amanda touched her mother lightly on the shoulder and pulled her aside, leaving Mrs. Chapman to gaze out at the view and try to catch a word or two.

"Mom, you could have at least told me he was drinking."

"What?"

"Dad. Why didn't you tell me?"

"Oh my." Mrs. Easton's fingers wrapped around her pearl choker that had been rinsed pink by the years. "Well, dear, I didn't know. But I'm sure it's just because it's such a special day. I'm sure it's nothing to worry about." She smiled hopefully at her daughter. "Everyone is saying how beautiful you look."

Amanda nodded, there was nothing else she could do, nothing else she had ever been able to do, she nodded and walked away. Only this time she found Sam.

"Jeez," he said. "Maybe you were right."

"Sam, I'm really sorry."

"It's okay. He seems to have lightened up. Sally's got him in the hallway playing with Maggie."

"Let's go before he makes a complete mess of things."

He looked for a moment at the shifting of her face and then he took her in his arms. "C'mon," he said firmly. "We'll go say good-bye to everyone and split."

"But sweetie," his mother protested, "why would you want to leave so soon? It's such a fun party."

"I know, Mom. But we're both tired. We didn't get much sleep last night."

"Leave the boy alone," Mr. Chapman said good-naturedly. "If I had a wife like that, I'd want to be alone with her too."

Mrs. Chapman frowned at her husband. "Well, we'll have all day tomorrow." She kissed them both good-bye.

Sam and Amanda made their way slowly through the other guests and finally headed to Mrs. Easton, who was standing near the entranceway.

"Thanks for everything, Mom."

"Of course. It was lovely, wasn't it?"

Sam nodded. "Thank you, Mrs. Easton."

Mr. Easton, coming down the hallway, saw his daughter and her new husband standing by the front door with his wife—she was his wife, wasn't she? he couldn't quite remember—and he walked over to join them. There was a leprechaun grin across his face as he wished them all the luck and love in the world.

"And luck," he added.

"You already said that, Dad."

He rolled his eyes at Sam. "See what you're in for?"

Amanda frowned and kissed him good-bye, and then she kissed her mother lightly near the ear, breathing in the Chanel No. 5 that had been the smell of adulthood to her all those early years when her mother would come home from a dinner party, the theater, a dance, and check on her in bed, smelling of the cold and fur and cigarettes and perfume. That's what it must be like to be grown-up, Amanda had thought, that's what it must be like.

The room pretended to be the same. The light fell just as it always did at this hour, spreading a few pale inches across the dying aloe plant, the morning paper was still on the table, folded in quarters to the crossword puzzle, and no additional words had been penciled in, the dirty dishes were still dirty, the couch still held the imprint of someone's seat. An imposter of a room, a sham, pretending nothing had changed.

Sam and Amanda collapsed onto the couch, exhausted, though it was only five-thirty and the evening still lay spread before them, waiting to be opened.

He lay back with his head against the wall and she went with him, finding the nook in his neck and kissing it before resting quietly on his shoulder. He ran his fingers lightly up and down her forearm.

"What do you think is going to happen to him?" he asked softly, carefully.

"Who?"

"Your father."

Amanda's chest rose and fell with her breathing. "You mean in general, or just tonight?"

"Either."

"I don't know. It certainly looks like last year's flirtation with AA bit the dust. As far as tonight goes, he'll probably just disappear."

"What do you mean, disappear?"

"He leaves. Or at least he used to."

"For how long?"

"A few hours. A couple of days. It depends. I don't think he wants to be around my mother when he's like that. It's like he thinks if it happens someplace else it doesn't really happen."

"Where does he go?"

Amanda shrugged. "I've never figured it out. I used to think he had a totally separate life hidden away someplace." She laughed and it was a foreign and oblique sound to Sam; like the occasional sad half-smile that sometimes landed on her mouth, it seemed to come from a different country. "Now of course, he does."

"Huh?"

"Joan, remember. The woman he married last year."

He cringed at the way she said it, the woman he married.

"Anyway," Amanda continued, "he certainly couldn't go there drunk. She was the one who got him dry to begin with."

"What does your mother do?"

"Christ," Amanda said, hitting him lightly on the thigh, "what is this, a pop quiz?" But then she went on. "Waits. My mother waits. And then when he comes back, which he always seems to do, she just steps aside and lets him in. That's what she does."

He turned her head to his and he kissed her and kissed her more but it tasted like some kind of sympathy and she pulled away.

"Your parents seemed to enjoy themselves," she said. "Is your mother always that gregarious?"

Sam laughed. "Always. They're so funny. They kept saying what an easy time they had finding the apartment. They really do think New York is like the Bermuda Triangle, swallowing the innocent for dinner."

"You mean it's not?"

"Anyway, they're giving it their best shot. This kind of thing is still hard for them."

"What kind of thing?"

122

"The way we got married. My mother actually asked me if we were doing it this way because we had to."

Amanda laughed. "You mean she thought I was knocked up?"

"That's the way she thinks."

"Wonderful. What did you tell her?"

"I told her you wanted to have a big church wedding with fifty-three bridesmaids and a chorus of castrati but your parents couldn't afford it."

Amanda laughed and kissed him and then sat back. The room was very quiet.

"So now what do we do?" Sam asked.

"Buy a condominium, have two children and get a divorce."

"That's fine for our long-range plans, but I was thinking about tonight."

"I don't know," she said.

They hadn't planned on this, this night like a universe before them, as wide as the future slapping at their feet, their cheeks, and they began to flail within it, looking for ways to hold it back, looking for something familiar.

"Are you hungry?" Amanda asked.

"No. You?"

"No."

Sam sat up and straightened his pants leg and they both watched.

"I know this sounds crazy," Amanda volunteered, "but do you want to just go to the movies?"

He was smiling when he turned around. "Sure."

"Great. Why don't you look in the paper and I'll go change."

"Don't."

Her hand poised mid-button. "Huh?"

"You look so pretty in that dress."

Amanda laughed. "You should have told me you go for this feminine stuff."

"See?"

"Okay, okay. I accept the compliment. And by the way, you look incredibly handsome yourself."

Sam and Amanda went to the movies in their wedding clothes, both careful not to touch themselves or each other when their hands grew greasy from the giant popcorn that they held between them. The movie, an idiotic teenage beach escapade in dolby sound, was one that they had spent the summer carefully avoiding. But tonight, their laughter grew in maddened circles and strangers' eyes darted through the darkness to see where it was coming from. They kissed with greasy lips.

They were still laughing when they slid out of the theater and began to make their way home.

"So tell me," Sam said as he steered her around a corner, "where did your family dig up that judge?"

Amanda laughed and squeezed his waist. "Transylvania?"

They paused for just a second when they came to a street light flashing its red-lettered warning and then they both began to run across the avenue just inches ahead of the oncoming traffic. It was hard to slow down when they got to the other side.

"Sam?"

"Yes?"

"I'm glad we did it."

He stopped and wrapped his arms about her and they stood still in the middle of the block. "Me too," he said. "Me too," and they kissed while a couple of teenage girls giggled from the stoop they had cluttered up with beers and magazines.

"C'mon," Amanda said.

They undressed side by side and Sam carefully hung up his suit in the back of the closet. Amanda watched from the bed while he picked her dress from its pale silken pond on the floor and hung it up and it made her smile, someplace inside everything else, and then he finally came to her. She slid her leg beneath his, it was a way they had, crooking knee to knee, it was what came first, and he made room to let her in. "I love you," she whispered into the caverns of his ear so that he could feel it echo all the way down.

"I love you too." And he slanted his eyes, his cheek, his mouth to her and she found him, found him as their mouths joined, lower and lower, joining, and he found her, here, in the back of her throat, the small of her back, joining, in and in and in, joining on the dank musky new soil that was theirs and theirs alone, in and in and in, pretending nothing had changed.

It was an hourless steel gray outside, filled with the kind of hard late summer rain that has no beginning and no end, that cures nothing and promises nothing except to go on and on.

"I don't see why you had to invite them here," Amanda grumbled as she wiped the crumbs of yesterday's toast off of the table.

"They wanted to see where we live. It seemed like a reasonable request."

"I guess. But . . ."

"Stop worrying. They're not expecting the Taj Mahal. Are you this bad when your parents come to visit?"

"They've only been here once, when I first moved in four years ago."

"Figures."

Amanda frowned. "I'm going in to dress. Will you take the cheese out of the refrigerator?"

"I already did."

"Figures."

Sam smiled. "Amanda?"

"Yes?"

"You already are dressed."

"I know. But I changed my mind."

"Oh."

Sam went into the kitchen and stared once again at the multitude of packages piled up in the refrigerator and on the counters. Amanda had spent over an hour this morning wandering from store to store, unsure what one bought when one's in-laws were coming at two in the afternoon. She had asked three different salespeople in three different stores if they thought that meant brunch or lunch or cocktails or tea and then she had bought something for each variable and dropped it all at Sam's feet. He was still trying to make sense of it when the intercom sounded.

Mr. and Mrs. Chapman stood in the doorway smiling and breathless from the three-flight walk, dripping onto the painted wooden floor. "What a time we had getting here," Mrs. Chapman said as she handed her flowered umbrella to Amanda. "Well they say rain at a wedding is good luck. I suppose the next day counts too. Anyway, we can pretend it does."

Sam shook hands with his father and kissed his mother before leading them into the living room.

"What a cute little place," his mother said as she sank deep into the couch. "I agree completely, it's much better not to clutter up a small place with too much furniture." Amanda smiled and nodded, wishing that she had bought some chairs, a rug, plants, anything.

"So what can we get you to eat?" Sam asked. "Mom? Dad?"

"Nothing, thanks," Mr. Chapman said. "We just finished lunch up at the hotel." He patted his flat stomach through his thin yellow pullover. There was a single drop of rain drying slowly on the top of his balding head.

"What we really want," his wife said, "is to get acquainted. We had so little time yesterday, and you know Sam, he left out all of the details." She reached over and fondled Amanda's knee. "Now tell us all about yourself."

Mr. Chapman rolled his eyes and Sam did too but this wasn't between them.

"I hear you work in a clothing store?"

Amanda smiled wanly. Let them think I am sweet and simple, she prayed, Sam's sweet and simple wife, how much easier that will be. "Yes, in the Village."

"How nice. Sam's last girlfriend worked with children. Do you get a discount?"

"On most things."

"Of course, we could tell just by looking at you that you'd be interested in fashion."

Amanda tugged at the hem of her longest skirt.

"Speaking of jobs," Mr. Chapman interrupted. "Sam, why don't you show us a copy of that magazine you write for?"

"I told you Dad, I don't do much writing anymore. I'm an editor now."

"Well then let's see a copy of that magazine you edit."

"To tell you the truth, I don't think we have one around."

Amanda didn't look at him, she didn't look at the pile of magazines in the corner, where the latest *Backlog* lay beneath yesterday's paper, she tried not to look anyplace at all.

"I'll send you a copy," Sam said.

"We've been waiting for that for some time now. You know how much we used to enjoy seeing your name in the *Ledger*."

Sam nodded and got up to refill his coffee.

"Come," Mrs. Chapman said as she hoisted herself from the couch, "show me the rest of the apartment."

Amanda rose and led her to the small bedroom in the back with its carefully made bed and lowered shades, and then into the bathroom and then there was no place left to go.

"Our first place was tiny too," Mrs. Chapman said as they reentered the living room. "Of course, as soon as you start your family, you'll probably want to leave the city anyway, right? I can't imagine who would want to raise children in New York."

Sam watched as Amanda simply smiled, shrugged. He had seen many of her wrappings before but he hadn't

128

seen this, this demure and deferential coating. "Mom, I told you, Amanda was raised in the city."

Mrs. Chapman smiled. "Of course, I didn't mean, but, well times are different now, don't you think?"

"Times are always different," Mr. Chapman offered.

"Maybe I will have something to eat after all. Since you went to all this trouble." Mrs. Chapman filled up a plate with an assortment of food and settled back onto the couch.

"So what did you two do last night?" Sam asked as he watched her carefully peel off a piece of wax from her cheese.

"Well, there was this game, ten innings it went," she paused to savor the memory.

Sam laughed. "You spent the night in New York watching a ball game on TV?"

"You should see her," Mr. Chapman said, laughing. "Double how she used to feel about basketball and maybe you've got this new baseball thing in mind."

"It was an important game," Mrs. Chapman replied. "Besides, we were both tuckered out from the afternoon. Your parents did it very nicely," she said to Amanda. "Of course, we wish we had more time to get to know them too. I guess they had all those other guests to look after. Somehow I kept seeming to lose place of them just when I thought we'd be able to settle in for a chat. Anyway, I invited them to Ohio for a visit."

Amanda didn't see Sam's reaction, she was staring at a piece of dust in the corner that she had missed.

"Tell me about Aunt Dora," Sam said. "I've been meaning to ask you what happened with her night school classes."

Every answer was greeted quickly by another question— he was good at it, he was very good at it—and none of it had anything to do with him, with her, with them, he was very good at it, and she was glad, this rainy afternoon, of his skill.

It was after five when Mr. Chapman finally glanced down at his watch. "We really should be going," he said. "We're taking an early flight in the morning and we haven't even packed."

"Packed," Mrs. Chapman complained. "There's nothing to pack."

"Come on, Pat."

"Okay," she said petulantly.

Sam picked the flowered umbrella off of the kitchen floor and handed it to his mother.

"This wasn't nearly enough time," Mrs. Chapman said as she kissed good-bye. "I expect you two to come for a nice long visit. When can we plan on it?"

"As soon as we get some vacation time, Mom."

"I'm taking that as an oath."

They closed the door behind them and listened as they began to walk slowly down the stairs.

"So what do you think?" Sam asked.

"About what?"

"My parents." He was a kid at show and tell, turning them this way and that.

"They're very nice."

Sam laughed. "Yeah," he said, "they are."

The rain had worn away into a moody mist and Sam and Amanda made their way through it hand in hand. They were a Léger couple now, outlined in black, set in relief against their past, and they found themselves practicing all of the polite solicitations of fellow travelers— glancing sideways at every tick, every sound, wondering how it would fit in, is that okay with you? yes, fine thank you, and you?

With each step, each block that they passed, they seemed to be leaving behind another fragment of the long weekend, fathers and mothers, unopened presents, unanswered questions, the smiling that had begun to dent their cheeks, they were walking further and further away from it, aimlessly, hopefully, and that seemed destination enough.

The West Village streets were filled now with the last of the summer tourists and tumblers and madmen and partiers looking for a final fling at the season, something to embellish in the cold months, looking for a way to make it last. The soggy streets pulsed with it, this last dose of energy, as laughing strollers tiptoed across the dark puddles, looking for someplace to go. At the outdoor cafés, a few brave people had wiped off the metal chairs and were sipping at cappuccinos and wine and pretending to be dry.

Sam and Amanda let themselves be pulled in by the music of a small jazz club that they sometimes enjoyed, but it was dense tonight with too many refugees and they could hardly hear the three-piece combo squeezed onto the small stage. They were halfway up to the bar when Sam turned to Amanda. "You don't really want to stay here, do you?"

She smiled. "No. Not at all."

But the idea of music had taken hold of them and they began to wander from club to club, studying the marquees and counting their money to see if they had enough for the cover charge and drinks. Here? No, not here, not tonight, another time then, thank you anyway, here?

It had begun to rain once more and they huddled beneath Sam's foldable umbrella until they came to a large empty bar and went in. In the back, there was one lost heavy metal kid on stage, his face and shoulders buried beneath his long blond frizzed hair, yanking early Led Zeppelin out of his electric guitar. Sam and Amanda settled onto a couple of rickety stools at the end of the bar's sparse lineup of sad and stupefied men playing air guitar along with the kid, nodding out, sleeping it off, staring into their own glazed eyes in the opposing mirror. In the corner, abandoned video games flashed orange and black and green and the bartender stood hunched by a reading light studying the racing form.

When the boy on stage slid abruptly into a medley of Kiss's greatest hits, Sam started to laugh. "What the hell are we doing here?" he yelled at Amanda.

"Beats me," she yelled back, and before the bartender had even noticed them, they left. Not here either, not tonight, another time perhaps, but not tonight, where then?

They headed east next, it was early still, past a group of kids by the University, unpacking carloads of cartons and stereos and clothes and all those dammed-up hopes strung together with graying ropes and they both smiled—it didn't make them feel old or wise or sad, they just didn't feel like kids.

Finally, on Second Avenue, they came across a corner jazz club that they had always meant to try—another night perhaps—and they went in gladly and found two seats at the bar. It was filled up with young men and women in colorful strapless party dresses, shaking the rain from their hair, checking themselves out in the silver wall that wasn't quite a mirror, eyeing each other with a determination loosened by the last-summer-night blues. On stage, a five-piece band jammed on and on, sometimes finding a melody and running away with it, and the man playing sax had an ageless used-up face.

Sam and Amanda drank their beers quietly. She watched him watching the band and she wrapped her arms about his neck and kissed him slow and slower.

"Careful," he said, smiling. "You're going to embarrass me in public."

They ordered another beer and let it thread, unthread, thread, around them. The women who had come in twos and threes still clung together and pretended to pay attention to each other or to the band or to the rain that fell like oil down the thick glass windows, to anything but the men, making their way deliberately past them, pretending to go to the bathroom, to the bar, not pretending at all, it was beginning to grow late.

"So what do you think?" Amanda asked. "Should we divide and conquer?"

Sam smiled and continued tapping his foot unconsciously in perfect rhythm with the band. The drummer had rolled up his sleeves and the tail of a tattooed dragon swung from the cuff.

The girl on the stool next to Amanda gave her long dark hair a sudden violent flip off of her bare shoulder and it slapped Amanda like a fan.

"Sorry," the girl said. But she turned quickly back to her perch when the movement had its desired effect and the guy in the tight jeans and the black T-shirt began to come her way, the guy she had rearranged her legs for, and her mouth.

He kept his eyes on her as he approached—Amanda and Sam were watching him too—and when he was very close to her, he took an extra step closer.

"Can I buy you a drink?" he asked and he made the question last longer than a dream.

The girl held up her full glass. "I'm fine." Her mouth was poised in a wet half-pout.

They watched him look her up and down and up, they listened as he said, "Yes, I can certainly see that." His eyes were high and bright as the Eiffel Tower. "You've got to be the prettiest girl in here." He set his drink down next to hers, the lips of their glasses touching. "What's your name?"

She thought for a moment before answering and Sam and Amanda couldn't help but lean a little closer. "Gina. What's yours?"

"Michael. So, Gina, what do you do when you're not sitting on barstools and looking delicious?"

Sam leaned far into Amanda's neck and it almost covered his laughter as he whispered, "See what I saved you from?"

She was laughing too. "We saved each other," she whispered back.

PART THREE

He ran his hands over the sanded edges and breathed in the gentle smell of freshly cut wood and it was all the Ohio afternoons in the garage to him, all the afternoons of planning and cutting and piecing together, all the promise of new projects. Already, he had poured his boxes from the back of the closet into the file cabinets the slab of wood rested on, carefully lining up his papers and his notebooks, his canceled checks, his canceled stories, his out-of-date résumés and his newly bought looseleafs waiting to be filled, waiting. He flipped slowly through their barren pages.

Amanda walked back into the bedroom and was jarred by the sight of her dresser now squeezed into a far corner, cockeyed and dusty, the new penny man at his new penny desk, and it pleased her with its shininess. Only the sound of him quickly shutting the cabinet drawer when he sensed her approach tricked her back. She went and wrapped her arms about his neck and kissed the top of his head. They used the same shampoo now and his hair smelled exactly like hers. "Hi."

He swiveled around and kissed her left breast and then her right. "Hi."

Amanda glanced over Sam's head at this desk, lined with perfect stacks of paper and unsharpened pencils in a new cup and erasers all in a row and she began to laugh.

He pulled away and smiled. "What are you laughing at?"

"Nothing."

"Nothing." He did a cartoon take on her voice, he was smiling still.

She kissed him again on the crown of his head. "You're so neat it astounds me. What an organization man."

He patted her behind and turned her head to her dresser with its bottles lying on their sides and three days' worth of clothes waiting to be hung up, to be washed. "One of us has to be," he said.

She laughed. "Well keep it up, toots. You're setting a fine example. Who knows, one day I may even try to follow it."

"Only in my dreams."

"I certainly hope you have more interesting dreams than that."

"I don't think we've been getting enough sleep lately to dream much. Anyway, what time is tonight's shindig?"

Amanda laughed.

In the two months since their wedding, they had both found a need to be out, for distraction, for movement, as if they were holding back with all hands the time when they would take it for granted, when it would be ordinary, when it would be it, their lives. They needed a background, incidental music to the real activity, the gradual knitting together of their lives, the unwrapping, the joining.

"I think if we go about ten, that should be okay," Amanda said.

"What do you want to do about dinner?"

"I don't care. How about Indian?"

Sam laughed. "What are the chances that the answer to that will ever be, 'Let's stay home and cook'?"

"When you divorce me and marry Betty Crocker."

"Right."

He kissed her before she walked away to change, holding a red dress and then a black one before her naked body while he watched. "Which one?"

"I don't know. They both look fine."

"You're no help."

"Okay. The red."

"You think?" She looked at them both again and slipped the black over her head. "I think this is sexier."

"Just who are you trying to look sexy for?"

"You, darling, only you."

Sam smiled and shook his head.

After dinner—Indian after all—Sam and Amanda walked the eight blocks to the new club, the new night. A small semicircle of people had gathered about the velvet ropes of the entranceway and Amanda smiled at the doorman as he waved them in.

"He's an old friend," she said as the rope went up behind them.

"Somehow that doesn't surprise me," Sam answered.

Inside, the large single room was dripping with carnival streamers and bunches of hanging plastic fruit. A samba band filled the small stage with its drums and swiveling hips.

"What is this, one night in Rio?" Sam asked.

Amanda smiled and took his hand, leading the way through the clusters of people as her eyes drifted from face to face, from wall to wall. Sam watched it, this scanning, this quick needle radar, as he had watched it so many nights before, vaguely disturbed by the restlessness and the hunger.

"Why do you always do that?" he asked now as they made their way to a long table that promised a couple of empty seats.

"Do what?"

"Scout the room like that. Who do you think you're going to find?"

They sat down and pushed aside some sticky glasses.

"It's not that."

"Well then why do you do it?"

Even in the pink and blue light he could see her redden. "I just like knowing where the fire exits are," she said, and began to look around for a waiter.

As they paused to order their drinks, he thought, always, always there is her fear of entrapment, always, she is looking for a way out.

But when the waiter left them behind, she turned to him and said, "Once, I saw a girl burn. It was in a club and the flashpots from the band's act exploded onto the dance floor. Her clothes melted onto her body and then disintegrated until she was standing naked in the room."

He ran his fingers down the slope of her neck and settled his hand on the back of her chair. "Jeez."

Amanda shrugged. "She was in shock. All she did was touch her head where her hair had burned off and scream, 'My God, what have you done to my hair?' "

He leaned over and kissed her, tucking this piece, this peel, deep into his back pocket. "What else?" he asked.

"What do you mean, what else?"

"What else haven't you told me?"

"What makes you think there are so many secrets?"

"Let's say it's my reporter's instincts."

Amanda smiled. "What else is there? The only thing that matters is that there's nothing in the whole damn world I'd rather do right now than dance with you."

Sam laughed. "Dancing your way out of hot spots?"

"Dancing my way into your heart."

"I think you're already there."

"I better be."

And they did, they danced in their own little off-beat way while other couples, couples who knew what to do, swirled and twirled and dipped about them, and when they danced, when it was the two of them, just the two of them amidst all the swirling others, the "us" of them, that was when they wanted each other most.

"Let's go home," Sam said.

"But we just got here."

"So what?"

Amanda smiled and nodded.

"What else?"

"I used to think I would die before I was eighteen," Sam said up into the middle blue night. They were lying nestled beneath a new, warmer quilt that they had bought together the week before, lying nestled within one of the middle blue nights that they had come to use for spelling it out, emitting sentences like smoke rings into the air and watching them rise, mingle, vanish—this unwrapping, this joining—a comfort strange and sweet.

"Why would you think that?"

"It wasn't just me. Everyone else thought so too. No one said anything, but they all thought so."

"I don't get it, Sam. Why?"

"Boys in my family did that." His feet wrestled beneath the sheets. "In the three immediate families, one cousin died of a brain tumor, one drowned in a neighbor's pool, all before they were eighteen. My family was next, I was the only boy. You see?"

"Kind of." She found his shoulder near her mouth and she kissed it and kissing had never been so easy.

Sam laughed. "Boy was I a mess at seventeen. I was convinced every cold was cancer, I looked four times before crossing every street . . ."

She ran her fingers down the smooth skin of his upper arm, up and down, lost in its curves, lost in the voice that she could feel echoing in his chest, thinking, this is why he became so wary of any form of uncertainty—

141

his caution had become a habit. "But you made it," she said. It sounded almost like a question.

"The funny thing is," Sam continued, staring at the ceiling, at the beginnings of a cobweb in the corner, "I was in a car accident a couple of months before my birthday. Me and Bobby McDonald went down a forty-foot ravine upside down in his jeep. We only stopped when we hit a tree. I'll never forget that feeling of flipping over, like it was in slow motion, happening to someone else."

Amanda shuddered. "Were you okay?"

"Bobby had a concussion and I needed some stitches in my knees. We were lucky. The first thing the state police said when they found us was, 'You deserve to be dead.'"

"How tactful."

Sam took her in his arms, but he was still lost in the shadows and the cobwebs of the ceiling. "I'll tell you something weird. It was one of those fluke accidents where if we had been wearing seat belts, we would have been decapitated. And I was so careful that year that I always wore seat belts. Just that once, I forgot." He paused and she could feel him inhale, exhale, she didn't know if it was him or her. "Who knows what you're supposed to believe in?" he said finally.

"Who knows?" she echoed.

She snuggled in closer, rubbing her cheek against his, closer, so that the bristles on his face scratched her skin. "I'm glad you made it," she said quietly.

Sam smiled, came down off of the ceiling, came to her. "Me too," he said. There was this comfort strange and sweet.

When they kissed, their tongues sought the ground that was theirs and theirs alone, sought to discover what they had brought home with them.

"Sam?" Amanda asked as she pulled away and rested her head against his shoulder.

"Yes?"

"Are you still scared of dying?"

"Not like that. I just don't think about it much anymore. I don't let myself. I mean, what's the point?"

She said nothing, breathed into the hollow of his neck.

He stroked her hair absently. "Do you?" he asked.

She pursed her lips, let it go. "Yes."

"Why?"

"I don't know. I always have. I think about it all the time. What it will feel like, how it will happen. I think about it every night before I go to sleep."

He continued with her hair, her cheek.

"Except lately," she said, "lately sometimes I forget to think about it."

And when they were inside of each other, for that is where they sometimes found each other, found it, when they were inside of each other and it was slower than the slowest sea until they could not bear it and when he quivered as he came and she knew the quiver and loved it all the more for knowing it, and when he could feel her contract about him, that was all the sense it had ever made to either of them. He pulled slowly out of her and kissed her and closed his eyes.

A few minutes later, Amanda sat up with her back to Sam and, quietly as she could, she began to knock on the wooden night table, three times with her right hand, three times with her left, three times with both hands together.

Sam kept his eyes closed as he listened. He had heard it before, this ritualistic pattern she performed, sometimes on chair legs under a table, sometimes here, in the night, always in complicated sets of three, always hidden, and he wondered once again what the bargain was, what she was so desperate to keep at bay.

She checked the register one more time, and the American Express forms and the petals of the flowers on their last good day, and then she started again, counting the change in the register, aligning the corners of the charge forms . . .

"Hi." Nancy walked in and headed straight to the back.

"Hi." Amanda waited a second or two before following.

Nancy was pouring herself a cup of the coffee that Amanda had just brewed and sliding out of her coat at the same time. When she had managed this, she carried her mug over to her desk and began to go over yesterday's receipts and then the pad with her list of things to do while Amanda watched.

"So," she said at last as Nancy crossed off the first two items, "there's something I've been wanting to talk to you about."

"Oh?" Nancy was staring at item number three, unable to remember what her shorthand referred to.

"Well. I've been thinking. Nancy, I think we should have more of a point of view here."

"Nipples," she muttered.

"What?"

"I need to buy more nipples for the bottle. What were you talking about?"

"The store. I think we need more of a sense of direction here."

"Huh?"

She tried to rein it in, edit out any edges, anything that might sound like criticism. "Just well, I think we could be more focused. We're trying to appeal to too many different tastes."

"I'm not sure I see what you're getting at."

"It's just, we need more of a, I don't know, something to make us more unique."

"I don't remember the *Times* commenting on that in their write-up last year."

"Okay. Maybe I'm not saying this right. But you did tell me you wanted more of my input."

Nancy nodded imperceptibly. "Well you're being so vague. Give me some specifics."

"Okay. I have this idea. I haven't worked out all of the details yet," she paused, looked at Nancy. "I thought we could do that together."

"Go on."

"Okay, look. Between the two of us, we know an awful lot of artists. I'm sure Deirdre does too . . ."

Nancy put down her pencil and laughed. "We are not opening up a gallery. There are at least seventy-five on this block already."

"That's not what I mean. What I thought was, how about if we try to get them to design some jewelry for us. It might be fun for them and it's something that could be just ours. An exclusive."

"And just how do you plan on financing this?"

"Well, I thought we could get them to do it on consignment at first. We'd pay for materials and we could guarantee them lots of publicity. I'm sure we could at least get *Backlog* to cover it. And then we'd take it from there. What do you think?"

Nancy played with the top page of her pad for a moment. "You really have given this some thought, haven't you?"

Amanda fidgeted as if caught in a lie.

"You really think you could talk some of the artists into it?"

"I don't know. It's worth a try, isn't it?"

Nancy smiled, shook her head. "Marriage sure is doing wonders for your attitude."

"Give me a break."

"No, I mean it. I don't think I've ever seen you this gung ho about anything."

"Does that mean you'll try it?"

"Well, it does sound like a good idea. Why don't you put some feelers out, see what kind of reaction you get, maybe some sketches, and bring them in."

"Okay, great."

"Amanda?"

"Yes?"

"Have you gotten any kind of commitment from *Backlog* about this?"

"Well, actually, I haven't had a chance to talk to Sam about it yet."

Nancy laughed. "I take it back. Marriage hasn't changed you all that much after all."

Amanda laughed too. "Yeah it has."

"Oh?"

But Amanda had already walked away.

On her way home that night, she stopped in a stationery store and bought three different sizes of pads and charcoal pencils and two Rapidographs and a new date book and even some graph paper, though she had no idea what she needed it for. At the last minute, she added a large black leather portfolio to her purchases. It took her two huge shopping bags to get everything home.

"**M**ark?" Sam leaned deep into his phone, as if talking to a mistress or a dealer, his back to the full office, his voice low. "Do you have a minute?"

"Sure. What's up?"

"Well, I've been thinking about that treatment . . ."

"Christ," Mark interrupted. "You didn't change your mind now, did you?"

"No."

"Good. Because it's too late."

Sam twirled his pencil, riddled with tooth marks, between his fingers. "I know that. And I wouldn't change my mind anyway. You know damn well I'm not about to quit my job."

"So what about the treatment?"

"Well I was just thinking that, you know that scene where the main character keeps calling and calling and can't get ahold of the girl?"

Mark was quiet and Sam didn't know what the silence meant except to go on.

"Anyway, I don't think he'd just give up after that. I think he'd find a way to go get her. Maybe he'd run for a bus, a train, but he'd find a way to get to her." The sentences were rushing out of Sam, looking for a home. "You see, that's the whole point, isn't it? His determination. That's what should be developed, so that the rest of it makes sense. Don't you think?"

"What I think is that you can't have it both ways."

"Huh?"

"Sam, you gave us your answer. You said you didn't want anything to do with this."

"I didn't say that. I said I couldn't do it full time."

"Same thing. The point is, I appreciate your interest, but you can't call up at this stage and tell us what to do with the script."

"I'm sorry. I just thought it was important. I thought you'd want to hear my ideas."

"I want to hear our scriptwriter's ideas. Look, I don't mean to be abrupt, but like I said, this is an either/or proposition, was, I should say, and you said no. Didn't you?"

"I did."

"Okay, then."

"Okay." Sam pulled at his hair and then lowered his hand to the desk. "I should get back to work. Deadline's on Thursday."

"Well, take it easy."

"Yeah, you too."

Sam hung up the phone and returned to the piece he had been editing, a bulimic's guide to the best restaurant bathrooms in New York. Photographs of the facilities accompanied the copy and he spread them out on his desk next to the neatly typed paragraphs—he hadn't touched them yet. Now he stared blankly at the captions for ten minutes before standing up and growling, "Where's John?"

He walked over to the front receptionist. "Where is he?" he demanded. "Why isn't he at his desk?"

"You looking for me?" John asked as he walked away from the men's room.

"I thought I told you I wanted some diners, some real greasy spoons in that piece. Not just Lutèce and Le Cirque."

"I didn't think it was a good idea. It doesn't fit."

"First of all, that's the point. Contrast. Second of all, I don't care what you think. I'm the editor."

"Jesus, if it's that important to you, Lucy and I will go out again this afternoon."

"Good. I want the copy tomorrow."

"Fine."

Sam went back to his desk and he didn't feel any better. He pushed aside the copy and the photos and got out his notebook and he scribbled into it for a few minutes but he still didn't feel any better. He went over to John's desk.

"I'm sorry. I shouldn't have snapped like that."

"It's okay, man."

"Okay."

He went back to his own little corner and waited until it was time to go home.

When he walked in the door, Sam came upon Amanda, sprawled out on the living room floor with a half a stationery store about her.

She looked up like a kid covered with fingerpaint. "Hi."

"Hi. What are you doing?"

"A project. Nancy just agreed to it. At least she agreed to maybe agree to it. We're going to try to get a few artists to design jewelry for us. It's going to be mine, Sam. Something I can really work on. I have a million ideas. It all makes so much sense. I'm sure the jewelry itself will be wonderful, and it'll be lots of publicity for the store and the artists and I even think it'll be fun to do."

He looked down at her, looked at this enthusiasm expanding like a balloon, he watched it and tried to guess its size, its weight, it was that new.

"So what do you think?" Amanda went on. "Isn't it a natural for a feature in *Backlog*?"

"Christ," Sam said. "How should I know?"

"What do you mean, how should you know? You're the editor."

"Right." Sam hung up his jacket and went into the bedroom and Amanda stood up and followed.

"Is something wrong?" she asked.

"No. Just a bad day."

"What happened?"

"Nothing happened."

"Did you tangle with Patrick?"

"I told you, Amanda. Nothing happened."

She stuck the pen she had been holding behind her ear and the felt tip left blue skywriting across her cheekbone.

"Sam?"

"What?"

"I know that you don't like it when I bring it up. But I'm making plenty of money now. Enough for both of us for a while if you want to quit."

"I'm not going to live off of your money."

"Why not? I mean, isn't that the point?"

"What point?"

"The point of being married. That we help each other out. If you want to talk about points, what's the point of staying someplace you're unhappy?"

"People do it all the time."

"That doesn't make it right."

"I didn't say I was unhappy."

"You didn't say you were happy either."

"Amanda, I'm really not in the mood for this tonight, okay?"

She backed up. They could only watch each other and wait.

"You're right," he said. "It does sound like a good idea for a feature in *Backlog*. As soon as you have something firm, I'll talk to Patrick about it, alright?"

She smiled. "Alright."

"Now will you please come here. You haven't even kissed me hello. Two months of marriage and already you're taking me for granted."

She went up and put her arms around him. "I'll take you any way I can get you."

"Any way?"

"Any way."

There was a heartbreak in the building.

One flight up, the same sad song played over and over and over again. Sometimes, the mourner picked up the needle even before the last doleful notes had sounded and placed it down at the beginning again—and it was always midnight for the singer and his lady never did come back.

"Jesus," Sam exclaimed, looking up from his pages. "I wish I knew the girl who did this to him. I'd offer her vast sums of money just to go back so we could have one night of relief."

Amanda glanced up from her seat by the phone where she had surrounded herself with clippings and calendars and phone numbers.

"How's it going?" she asked.

"Okay." Sam brushed aside a pile of pencil shavings. "It's been a long time since I did a profile. It feels good to be writing again."

"What happened with the binge and purge piece?"

Sam smiled. "Lunch and hunch? It's done. This is something I'm actually going to do myself. On a choreographer. I thought I told you, we're supposed to go see him later this week."

Amanda nodded distractedly. "Fine," and began to dial the next artist on her list.

Sam returned to his notes, but he was really listening to her. ". . . and we thought since you did three-dimensional work you'd be perfect for the project. I'd love to come to your studio . . . next Thursday? That would be great . . . Yes, we're excited about it too . . . I am a little surprised that you already heard about it though . . . I guess so . . . Well, a little word of mouth can't hurt, right? Okay then . . .''

He was watching it, weighing it, he was waiting for her to be done, though he pretended to be absorbed in his own work when she reached over to hang up the phone.

"Do you know how old this guy is?" he asked accusatorily.

Amanda hardly looked up from the date book she was scribbling in. "Who?"

"The choreographer," Sam answered impatiently. "George. George Wilkinson."

"How old?"

"Twenty-four."

"So?"

"So he's already won three major grants, been on the cover of two magazines, performed all over Europe . . .''

Amanda looked at Sam. "Are you having trouble with the piece?"

"No. I told you, I'm glad to be doing some writing again."

"Good."

"It's just a little surprising to me that someone so young could accomplish that much."

"There have always been people like that."

"I know. I don't know. These transcripts are complete bullshit. When we were doing the interview, Patrick kept asking these incredibly inane questions."

"Like?"

"Like, what kind of underwear do you wear when you dance, how old were you when you lost your virginity, that kind of crap. As soon as we began to broach anything remotely serious, he threw in something like that."

Amanda nodded. She had only three names to go. "So why don't you just leave that stuff out?"

"You don't understand," Sam's voice was growing exasperated. "He's the managing editor."

"So don't leave it out."

"I did three nights' worth of research on modern choreography," Sam grumbled.

Amanda was growing frustrated. Also, she was suddenly rather curious about what dancers do wear under their leotards. It seemed like a good question to her. "I've got to finish these calls before it gets too late," she said, already beginning to dial.

Sam nodded and returned to his own pileup, staring at the redacted notes once more, trying to ferret out a lead.

"So anyway," Amanda was smiling across the room at the bookshelf, "what we were thinking was, you could just show us some sketches, I know you must be very busy, maybe if you had the time, you could do a few prototypes, but if not . . ."

Sam picked up his pencil and ripped a sheet of paper off his yellow legal pad to write Amanda a note: "Going out for coffee, be back in a little while, okay?"

He gathered up his things and held the note before Amanda's eyes, watching as she nodded without taking the phone from her mouth, and then he grabbed his jacket and left.

He walked down the three broad worn steps into the dimly lit café and wove between its narrow aisles until he came to a small empty table by the brick wall. He settled into a wavering balance on a wrought iron chair and sat with his coat on as he breathed in the undulating waves of reggae and the hiss of the espresso machine and the cat playing with a shredded napkin about the dusty floor. He eased into it, this place of his, this alcove in the city he kept only for himself, eased into the darkness and the warmth, into the cocoon of knowing no one, being unknown, eased into it like a shipboard romance, this balmy solitude of his. It took over ten minutes to be noticed by the waitress, a spindly bleached blonde who could not, with all the tattered black clothing, all the garish makeup in the world hide her translucent young skin.

Sam took off his jacket and pushed aside the clay bowl of sugar packets, the Perrier bottle with its dying white carnation, and spread his notes out on the shaky black table. All about were other people with other notes, or perhaps couples, lost in intimate conversations—surely their notes were more interesting, more important, surely their conversations more intense.

He took a sip of his espresso, thick and bitter, and finally picked up his pencil, winding it up and down the page, looking for the right line. The choreographer was twenty-four and . . .

Twenty-four. When he was twenty-four, he'd had them already, he'd had them forever, the walls, the walls that held him together and held him in, he had thought you needed them then, he still did, the walls that had sprung full-grown, impenetrable, the walls he defended even as he banged his head against them, and there didn't seem to be a way over or under or through them, even if he had sought it, did others have them too? surely not him, not this choreographer, twenty-four, these walls that had lately seemed to be built on such questionable foundations that it was impossible to discover what they were made of.

He shook his head, snapped the lemon peel into the tiny cup. The choreographer was twenty-four and . . .

"Well since we know you're not rewriting *Citizen Kane*, I'll have to assume you're still doing the fashion two-step."

Sam looked up and found Mark, grinning down at him. "Hi."

"Hi. Can I join you for a minute?"

"Sure." He cringed with it, the loud pop of his alcove being pierced and deflated about him.

"Good. I'm getting take-out but they're all backed up." Mark sat down and turned Sam's notes around so that he could read them. "So who's today's lucky star?"

"Some choreographer still in diapers."

"Is that an artistic statement or a bladder control problem?"

"Is there a difference?"

"Uh oh." Mark switched into the deep stentorian voice that could still be heard selling cars up and down the radio dial. "Disillusioned boy from small-town America . . ."

Sam laughed uneasily. "Shut up."

"I told you to get out of there," Mark continued, pushing away the notes. "I offered you a terrific project, a whole new riff, but did you listen?"

"If it isn't the quintessential out-of-work actor lavishing his advice on a lowly journalist."

Mark smiled. "Sorry. Actually, I'm glad I ran into you. I wanted to apologize if I sounded gruff the other day."

"That's okay. I understand."

"Do you? You know, I really was hoping you would go in on the project. And I think you wanted to do it too. But it was forbidden fruit to you, and that's what got me so frustrated. It was only forbidden because you wouldn't let yourself . . . See, it could have been a reality."

"What is this, Pop Psychology 101? We've been through this. I just didn't have enough security saved up to quit my job."

"Security isn't something you save up. It's something you find when you take risks."

"Maybe, maybe not. Anyway, I'm not in the mood to get into that all over again. How's it going?"

Mark smiled. "Well, I'm sure you'll be thrilled to hear it's going fantastically. We found some young hot-shot from the film department at Columbia and he's writing his little ass off. He's already come up with a plot device to . . ."

Sam nodded and played with the edges of his notebook and the walls were up and up and up and he stood teetering on the top peering down at one side and the other, stood teetering on the top, frozen. "Listen," he said during what seemed like a break, "I know you've got to get going and I really should try to pull this profile together."

Mark laughed. "The man with the connections, the drink tickets and the by-line."

"That's me, journalism's Renaissance man."

"Okay," Mark said, standing up. "But we should get together when we can have some time. Maybe with Amanda. Did I tell you I have a new girlfriend?"

"No, that's great. Okay, well I'll give you a call. That is, if you're still taking my calls."

"Only up until our first Academy Award."

"Well that should give me enough time."

"Bye."

"Bye, take it easy."

Sam waited until Mark had left with his take-out cappuccino and his swagger and then he climbed back, back in, shuffling his papers this way and that until he pushed them aside and found it, the dark red notebook buried underneath, always buried, found in it the stream of neat black handwriting that grew by itself as if someone had slit him open and imprinted his innards on the page like a bloody Rorschach test, found what he hid even from himself, and he began to write, climbing in, further in, as the reggae and the hissing steam and the other couples melted down until everything else, everything, even the endless miles and miles of walls, everything disappeared, for a little while.

The street was striped with people walking quickly through the chilling night and Sam walked quickly too, clutching his notebooks tightly to his chest, his eyes lowered, trying not to think of anything, anything at all, just walking, going home, just that. A few yards away, he got caught on a pair of fluorescent blue heels and his eyes stuck as they lifted and set down, lifted and set down, and at first it was only that, these fluorescent blue heels, and then there were the black opaque stockings, the short black skirt and leather jacket, the blond hair that flew from her head like a thick camp blanket, there was this woman ahead of him, but he wasn't thinking about her, only about walking, going home, only that, as the blue fluorescent heels lifted and set down.

He would never know her. This woman walking step by step away from him, so quickly, as he fastened his pace to hers, this woman with the blue heels with someplace to go that would never be his, a room, a lover, her blue heels clicking their way around the corner now, a corner that wasn't his—until he somehow found himself following, following them, following her.

Up the block then, not thinking about anything at all, not about walking, not about going home, not about going anywhere, just about these blue heels, this woman he would never know, walking by a jewelry shop now, her reflection gliding across the window, her angular face, her wan complexion offered back to her, offered for a vanishing instant to him. But he didn't want to face her, didn't want to know her, he only wanted to follow, for some reason to follow her, to see where she was going, which steps she would climb, to see the secrets in the arch of her foot, for she held that, the secrets of all the women he would never have, never know, all the strange women with their heels and their rooms and their lovers, the one forever out of reach, he followed, maybe it was her, with her blue heels and her black stockings and her room, maybe she held it, the secret, the key, the bulldozer of his walls, maybe it was her, he followed as she stepped carefully over a broken beer bottle, hardly looking down, searching for the secret in her stride, in the curve of her ass, in the back of her head that would never turn for him, the secret that he followed but was careful not to touch, he followed, wondering why nothing ever felt real to him, as she walked across it with her fluorescent blue heels, walked across the top of it, back and forth, and he followed even as another voice, growing steadily louder, was telling him that he was mad, it was mad, this, this following, so that when she rounded another corner, he let her go, let her go with all the sadness and remorse of a dimestore love story, and he pried himself around.

Sam had to walk four blocks back and start again, start home again, and he returned to his fast pace, his downward glance, tinted now by a smudgy wash of shame. Someone even more anxious to get home than he brushed into him and he jumped instinctively but he did not stop the way he used to. There were times when, for just an instant or two, he forgot where he was, forgot the city—and those were the only times he ever really felt at home. He crossed with the others, before the light had changed fully to green. The most he could hope for was to blend in.

Amanda had long since put away her notes and her date book. In the crawling and crawling time since he had left—gone out for coffee, be back in a little while, okay?—in the crawled-out time that he was gone, she had put on a lace slip because she knew it was the one he liked, had straightened the bed and poured herself a glass of wine, had found herself becoming more and more greedy for him, in the too much time when she didn't know where he was.

She heard the keys in the door and she went and stood before it so that he would find her there, find her first.

After a second, he smiled. "Hi."

"Hi. You've been gone so long. I was beginning to get worried."

"Sorry. I really wanted to stay until I finished the damn thing."

"Did you get it done?"

"It's going to have to wait until after we see his work."

"Oh."

He reached to kiss her, his wife, and she wrapped her arms gratefully around him, tasting the cold on his lips, tasting the outside of him, the otherness of him, taking it in her hands, her mouth.

"Let's go inside," he said.

He led her into the bedroom and he took her, took her slip and her want and her fragile sense of belonging, took her into him, leaving his notebooks and his coat and his jeans on the floor, he took her, and it was her, only her, except for an extra slab of hardness in him that was just for the woman in the fluorescent blue heels, and he knew it, and she knew it too, even if she didn't know the color.

And when he was certain that she was asleep, he picked the notebooks off of the floor and hid them in the back of his file cabinet.

"This week," Sally said, "we're only supposed to touch. It's hysterical. Frank gets this incredibly serious look on his face and of course he sticks exactly to the areas he's allowed to touch, like there's a map painted onto my body. I can't help it, I start to laugh every time, which of course just makes it worse, 'cause then he gets all aggravated and tells me how important this is and how I don't have the right attitude and that only makes me laugh more." Sally paused and took a bite of her grilled cheese sandwich. "Then," she continued, while still trying to coax a thin white thread of cheese into her mouth, "we go to the analyst and he tells on me. Really. He's like one of those kids you hated in grammar school. He's trying to be the analyst's pet."

Amanda laughed. "And is he?"

"Of course. I mean, I'm not about to tell those two what I really think. It's just too absurd."

"Sally, why are you bothering to go through all this therapy together if you're not going to tell him what you really think?"

"Well, I tried once. A couple of weeks ago, I said that the way he walked, you know how he hardly bends his knees? made me want to throw up. And the two of them just stared at me. Finally, the analyst said, 'Well that's just a symptom. That's not the real point, now is it?' " Sally lit a cigarette, a new habit for her, and for the first time the smoke irritated Amanda. "But the thing is," she said as she exhaled and tried to remove a nonexistent

161

piece of tobacco from her tongue, "I think that it is the point. I mean, if you can't stand the way someone walks, well . . ."

"Well?"

"I could have sworn I saw Frank tote up another point for himself. I knew we should have gone to a woman analyst. Anyway, we have one more night of touching exercises. Who knows? Maybe the root of the whole problem really is that I'm not in tune with the area just behind my left elbow. It makes about as much sense as anything else, right?" She put out her cigarette and went back to her sandwich. "If only he wasn't so damned serious about it. It makes him look like such a fool. So. Speaking of sex lives, how's yours?"

Amanda was still unused to this brassiness of Sally's, it wasn't natural the way it was with some of her girlfriends, but like a teenager's newfound strut, too self-conscious, too cocky. Nevertheless, she couldn't at this point say, None of your business.

"It's okay."

Sally laughed. "You mean the honeymoon's over already?"

"I said it was okay."

"There are a few thousand miles between okay and great," Sally said. "Or is it inches?"

Amanda smiled indulgently. "You know, it's funny," she said, "but I thought getting married would make sex better."

"What on earth gave you that idea?"

"I don't know. I just thought we would relax more, let go. That it would make us somehow freer."

"And?"

"And it's fine. It's just that it's exactly the same."

"You don't know the meaning of the word," Sally said drily. But then she smiled. "How long have you been married, two months?"

"Two and a half."

"Give it time. You're probably still getting used to each other. Have you tried talking about it with Sam?"

"There's nothing to talk about. I told you, it's really fine." She was suddenly ticklish, jittered by the show of any bruises, any sore spots that she had long ago learned to camouflage. Besides, everything was fine, better than fine, and when he held her in the night, when she thought about it in the day, knowing that he would be there, that they would be there together, and in the morning too and the next night, when she thought of that, it was better than fine, that knowing that almost took the guesswork out of nights, out of mornings. "So," she said, taking a bite of her sandwich. "What else is new?"

Sally smiled. "I had lunch with Dad last week."

"You're kidding me. What brought that on?"

"I don't know. He called me. He had gotten all teary-eyed at the wedding and I promised. Anyway, don't say anything in front of Frank, okay? I didn't tell him."

"Okay. So how was he?"

"Sober. Repentant. The usual. He told me he wants to divorce Joan, but he seems too scared to call her up and give her the good news."

"I think she's probably picked up on it by now."

"You'd think. Anyway, I still think Mom's a complete idiot to take him back."

"She loves him."

"Since when are you such a true believer?"

"I'm not saying she should or shouldn't let him stay. I'm just saying I understand it."

"I know. I do too. I just wish I didn't. Listen, Amanda, there's something else I wanted to talk to you about."

"Oh?"

"How are things going at the store?"

"They're good. To tell you the truth, we're having our best season yet." She didn't mention the jewelry project, for no particular reason, except that it was hers.

"That's what I thought."

Amanda sat up straighter in her chair.

"So what I was thinking was, during the holidays, you'll probably need some extra help, don't you think?"

"Well actually, we're pretty well covered."

"Oh."

"Look Sally, if I can do anything else. I mean, I'll try to think of some other people who . . ."

"Forget it. It was just a thought. We probably wouldn't get along working together anyway."

"It's not that. We just don't need anyone right now."

"Right."

They both stared at the crusts of their sandwiches.

"Do you want anything else?" Amanda asked.

"Huh?"

"Dessert. Did you want any dessert? Because if not, I should get going."

"No, that's okay."

Amanda motioned for the check. "Well, good luck at the therapist's tomorrow," she said as she took a bill out of her wallet. It was her turn.

"I'll need it. It's our last chance."

Amanda looked up at her. "What then?"

"Who the hell knows? I shudder to think what Plan B might be." Sally carefully reapplied her lipstick and then put the tube back in her purse. "You're lucky," she said.

"Why?"

"I can't imagine this happening to you and Sam."

"No?"

"No."

They kissed good-bye out on the street and Amanda walked quickly back to Legacies and there was only this, this knowing that he would be there in the night, in the morning—almost knowing.

The air had on its new sharp-
ness and they both kept
their hands in their pockets as they walked down Second
Avenue on their way to the performance in what was
once a public elementary school. There were fewer people meandering with no place to go now, and Sam and
Amanda made their way quickly down the wide avenue
as they talked in a desultory, quick-walking kind of way
about—what? Nancy's reluctance to stay open an hour
later, *Backlog*'s increasing circulation . . .

"Is Patrick meeting us there?" Amanda asked as she
sidestepped one of the vendors huddled protectively by
his stash of platform shoes and old *Playboys* spread out on
a blanket.

"No. You know him, he's interested in the idea, not
the fact. Besides, this is my piece."

"Good. Actually, I'm looking forward to seeing what
he's . . ." About halfway down the block, a small thin
man was heading toward them. He was wearing loose
khaki pants, sneakers, a black leather motorcycle jacket,
his coal black hair bedroom-messy, his large dark eyes
pushed deep into his lined and gaunt face—Amanda started.
"I don't believe it," she muttered.

The man seemed to notice her at exactly the same
moment, but if there was any surprise, it didn't show, not
in the slow confident gait, not in the satisfied smile that
seeped across his face. They had come upon each other
now, they were standing face to face.

"Tom," Amanda said, as if to verify.

"Hi." His voice too was bedroom-messy, confident and unsurprised.

They didn't kiss hello but reached instinctively to each other instead. He touched the sleeve of her coat, she could not help but finger aside a wayward strand of hair that had landed in his eye. Her fingers fell from his brow down across his sharp cheekbones and only gradually back to her side.

"How are you?" she asked finally.

"Good." There were no absent years in his voice, it was as close as if they had just seen each other yesterday, this morning, that close. He continued to smile at her. "You look great. You've let your hair grow."

Amanda touched her hair briefly, smiled back. "It's been a long time." She chewed the inside of her cheek. "Are you staying out of trouble?"

He laughed, at her, at himself. "As much as possible."

Amanda laughed too, an intimate laugh of memory and forgiveness. Suddenly though, she remembered that outside of them, there was Sam, standing impatient and perplexed by her side. "Tom. This is my husband." The words were large and rusty in her mouth.

Tom looked at Sam and smiled—this too he took in stride, his stride that nothing could break. "Hello."

"Sam," Amanda added as an afterthought.

"Hello, Sam." He seemed amused as he offered his hand. "Congratulations." Done with this, he turned back to Amanda.

"Well," they both said at once. There was a pause that neither was willing to break up with the usual patter of questions about jobs and acquaintances.

Tom turned back to Sam. "Take good care of her," he said. His smile, was it mocking, amused, smug?

Sam was still watching it when Amanda answered, "He does." His smile was exactly the same as hers, that's what it was.

The three of them stood in silence for another minute.

"Well," Tom said, "I've got to get going."

"You always did."

Tom laughed and leaned over to kiss her good-bye. "Angel," he whispered in her ear. He smiled at Sam and walked past them.

Sam and Amanda once again started walking in the direction of the old elementary school building, wordless for the next half a block.

"What did you say the name of the choreographer was?" Amanda asked as they waited for the light to change.

"I don't remember," Sam muttered.

"Oh."

"George something."

"Right."

They reached the large red door in silence and Sam gave his name at the card table that had been set up with a cigar box for money and ticket stubs. The woman crossed it off the complimentary list and they climbed the worn black steps, the cold stone still redolent of all the years of children's impatient feet, rolling laughter. They found two empty folding chairs in the back of the room.

They sat for a couple of minutes with the mimeographed programs resting unopened on their laps.

"I haven't seen him in six years," Amanda said finally.

"Oh."

They both stood up to let someone squeeze by them, sat back down.

"Are you going to sulk all night?"

Sam looked at her and smiled distantly. "No." He opened the program and began to read the dancers' biographies.

Of course, he knew that there had been other men. Hell, he was even friends with Bill these days. But this was different, for some reason different. The lights went out and three men took to the stage, or rather, walked out onto the floor. As recorded atonal music flooded the room, they began to leap about, their tie-dyed pants flap-

ping in the air, their bare feet landing with a loud, grace-
less thud. This was very different. It was his smile, that
goddam smile, knowing, taunting, it was the way they
had reached to each other, surely she had never reached
to him quite like that, it was the way he had said, "Take
care of her," and how she hadn't rebelled or laughed, but
understood, acquiesced . . .

The music was loud, grating.

But for Amanda, it could not drown out that softest of
whispers—Angel—that insidious warm breath that drifted
down her spine like smoke . . .

The two of them sat side by side in the dark, staring
blankly at the barefoot dancers with their dirty soles.

When they got home that
night, Amanda flicked on
the lights and kicked off her shoes with one motion.
Often, Sam tripped over the scattered collection of pumps
that ringed the front door for days at a time, until Amanda
had run out of shoes and was forced to pick them up.
Now he kicked them aside and started to walk to the back
of the apartment.

"Do you want a brandy?" Amanda asked.

"No."

"Sam?"

There were hours and hours before he answered. "Yes?"

She waited too. "I wish I had a clean slate to offer
you. But I don't."

He stopped in the hallway, walked back toward her.
"I know." His hand wrapped around the half-curl behind
his ear, the rest had been cut off last week. "I know. It's
just that he was so . . ." he sat down on the couch, "so, I
don't know . . ."

Amanda sat down beside him. "I know."

"Intense."

She laughed. "Yes."

"Who was he?"

"Just someone. I told you, it was six years ago."

"He looked like more than just someone to me,"
Sam said testily. "Were you in love with him?"

Amanda smiled. "It had nothing to do with love."

When Sam said nothing, she went on. "It was an odd
relationship."

"Odd?" The way they could not help but reach to each other. "In what way, odd?"

Amanda looked over at him, as if weighing what to describe, what to omit, she knew there was no real way to explain. But she wanted to make him see, really see, for the first time she wanted to try, he was her husband after all, try to see what it had been like, what she had been like. She plunged forward, not so much toward him but into her own shadowy recesses. "We spent a few months together," she said quietly. "It was always four in the morning."

"What does he do?"

Amanda laughed at the irrelevance of the question, at Sam, always struggling vainly to fit each piece into a perfectly formed cog—as if that would help. "Nothing. I don't know." She took a sip of the brandy she had poured for herself. "He grew up on the Lower East Side. He read dirty comic books and the *Tibetan Book of the Dead.*"

"You had a lot in common?"

She ignored the sarcasm. "Something. Something was the same in us." She pulled her legs tightly beneath her. "I guess we were both scared then."

"Of what?" Had he, this other man, somehow captured the fluttering that Sam could not help but shrink away from?

"I don't know. Weren't you ever just scared?"

"I told you I was."

"But that was something specific. I mean vague, four-in-the-morning scared."

Sam's eyes skidded from her kneecaps to the amber liquid swirling in her glass and landed at her feet. He didn't answer.

"Anyway," Amanda continued, "he loved women."

"So? A lot of men love women. I love women."

"Not like that."

Amanda stopped suddenly. This wasn't it, this wasn't it at all, it was something altogether different. How could she make him see? She changed her voice, her thread. "I used to have this beautiful antique gold necklace," she said, staring at a misplaced book on the shelf across from them. "It had an engraved locket, a single pearl on a sliding clasp. I think it was Victorian. Anyway, I used to wear it all the time. And he would finger it and say, 'Sooner or later, you'll hock it. You'll see. Sooner or later, you'll hock anything.' "

Sam uncrossed, recrossed his legs, said nothing.

Amanda smiled that same puzzling godforsaken smile but he did not see it. "He was right, of course. When I . . ."

Sam stood up abruptly. "Look, I'm tired," he said. "I think I'll go to bed."

Stunned, her sentences snapped in half with one clean break, Amanda watched as he walked purposefully away from her into the bedroom. She remained silent—whatever else she was going to say, offer him, lay aborted on the floor, dead and stinking. She did not call after him, yell for his return, insist that he listen to her, come back. She didn't say a word.

For the next couple of days, they skirted each other with a chary politeness, kept the arm's length distance of muted anger and regret. They had in common a fear of eruptions, of tears that could not be mended, and so they smiled when they passed each other in the hallway, they kept up a careful volley of small talk through dinner, they said please and thank you.

They did what could be done with perfectly valid excuses; perhaps they stayed a few minutes later at work—it was busy, after all; became increasingly absorbed in a certain book—I've been meaning to read it for years; suddenly had to see a friend—his girlfriend walked out on him, he needs me. And at night, they lay side by side and tried to keep from overlapping.

In fact though, there were a million split seconds when Sam started to turn to her, but whenever he sneaked a glance in her direction it was rebuffed by the cold shiny marble surface of her resentment, and he closed his mouth. Each night, despite his resolve, all that he could manage to say was, "Good night." And night after night, Amanda lay awake, waiting, until she was worn to a pale anxious rendition of herself, impatient and desirous finally not for any words from him but only for sleep.

On the third night, Sam called Amanda from work and said that he had to have dinner with Patrick and the choreographer to discuss the article. "Okay?"

"Fine."

It was the first full evening that she would have to

herself since their marriage and Amanda planned for it a ladder of small selfish pleasures that would hopefully lead her to sleep, relief. On her way home, she bought perfumed bubble bath and a vial of over-the-counter sleeping pills, she picked up a new album by a torch singer who Sam detested and a good bottle of Bordeaux, she planned on how good it would feel, to be alone.

But she hadn't planned on the words, still banging at her head, banging at Sam, hadn't planned that even beneath the blanket of the wine, the sweet white bubbles, her fists would still be clenched. She took one and a half of the little blue pills and washed them down with another glass of wine and she finally drifted off while the woman with the haunted voice went one last tango with a certain someone.

Sam came home stumbling drunk well after midnight. He did not turn on the lights but did an exaggerated mime dance of quiet, of solicitude, a clown's imitation of concern, tiptoeing slowly to bed, hushing himself when he squeaked—before he dove on top of her, his clothes, his shoes, still on. He wanted only to be gentle, to be loving—he had missed and missed her—as he tenderly kissed her cheeks, her eyes. She was in such a deep sleep that it took her a few moments to rise to the surface and find his cold wet mouth on hers.

"Hey," Sam tried to whisper in her ear. The scotch that he had finished the evening with bit through the last layer of sleep.

"Get off of me," Amanda hissed.

He did not hear her, or heard but didn't believe her, for he continued to kiss, or rather, move his soggy lips about her face.

Amanda jabbed him with her elbow. "You bastard," she sputtered. "Get off of me."

Sam stopped, looked down uncomprehendingly, then he sighed like a last-round loser and finally rolled away. He climbed clumsily off of the bed and began to swear in low slurpy stutters before plodding ostentatiously into the living room.

Amanda, of course, could not fall back to sleep, could not, despite the pills, the wine, her piled-up exhaustion, will herself back inside the slumber—he had ruined it. She was defeated, and furious, too furious to lie still, silent, in separate rooms. She kicked the warm covers off of the bed and went to find Sam.

"How could you have done that?" she demanded, standing over the couch he had collapsed onto, her hands on her hips.

"I just wanted to make love to you," Sam answered sulkily.

"You knew I hadn't slept in three nights, you knew all I wanted in the whole fucking world was to sleep."

"I'm sorry."

"You know what I've been like the past few days."

"Right."

"I mean, it's not like you tried gently or anything. No. You just crash right onto me. You didn't give a damn how I felt."

"Jesus, Amanda, I said I was sorry." His voice was exasperated, rung to cinders. He had only wanted to make love, to make up. "What more do you want?"

"You think that just because we're married I'm suddenly your property?"

Sam laid his head in his hand. "I don't believe this," he said, mostly to himself. And then to her, "No. That's not what I think."

She continued to glare at him. "Well?"

He exhaled loudly. "Obviously nothing I say tonight is going to make it any better." He began to sink further into the sofa, as if all of his muscles had suddenly left town. "So why don't we just go to sleep?"

"You bastard," Amanda said once again. But it didn't have the sword thrust it did before, for as she looked down at his collapsed body, she knew that she was losing her strength to fight his weariness, and her own too.

"You might as well come to bed," she said angrily.

He opened his eyes and stood slowly up, he moved sheepishly to embrace her.

"Don't even think about it," she muttered, stepping out of his reach.

Sam moaned when the alarm went off the next morning and pulled himself painfully from the bed. He looked over at Amanda, lying perfectly still, but he couldn't tell whether she was sleeping or not—he was scared to bend too close. In the bathroom, he swallowed three aspirin and then stood for a long while with his eyes closed beneath the hot pounding water of the shower. When he finally pushed aside the soap-filmed shower curtain, he found Amanda seated on the toilet, her elbows, her knees, her eyes, all folded in. He grabbed a towel and wrapped it tightly about his waist.

He was still bleary-eyed and unnerved and he couldn't, despite his attempts at keeping it usual, keeping it standard, find his razor, and so he reached back into the shower and grabbed hers. He lathered his face and began to shave, the light pink plastic razor in his hands felt as dangerous as everything else. He avoided looking over to see if Amanda was watching him or not.

"I'm sorry about last night," he said as he completed the first stroke and knocked the foam into the sink. "I was a jerk."

"I'm sorry too. I guess I overreacted a little." In fact, she had waked terrified that he would never again try to make love to her.

Sam continued to shave and Amanda pulled distractedly on a loose string of the face towel. Neither was satisfied.

"I was drunk," Sam said.

"No kidding."

"Look, maybe I went about it the wrong way, but I just wanted to, to hold you. It's been so fucking awful the last few days."

"I know. But you knew how I was feeling."

"I guess I forgot."

"I guess you did."

Sam rinsed his face with lukewarm water and took the towel that Amanda handed him.

"How could you have just walked away the other night when I was trying to tell you something?"

His face was buried in the towel. "It was late."

"Bullshit." She paused, as surprised as he at the unexpected screech of the brakes being applied. "Ever since we met," she went on, "you've done nothing but tell me that I'm not open enough with you, that I don't trust you enough. And then, when I try, when I try to tell you something, you walk away." She was struggling to keep her voice from cracking. "You only want to hear it if it's what you want to hear."

"I'm sorry," Sam said. He was standing now with his hands on the sink ledge, staring down into the soiled drops of water. "Don't think I . . ." he paused, took a deep breath. "It's all I've been able to think about," he said in a very low voice. "For days, all last night, all I've been able to think about is that goddam necklace of yours." He turned to her. "What happened to it?"

A small soft laugh fell out of Amanda. She had forgotten all about the necklace, it was no longer important, no longer real, it was no longer anything at all; the warm breath like smoke down her spine had disintegrated and it was no longer four in the morning—it hadn't been for such a long time. She smiled, dismissed it. "I'll tell you some other time," she said. "It doesn't matter."

Sam looked at her with confusion.

"Sam?"

"Yes?"

"I never loved anyone before I met you." It was simple and flat as truth. "I didn't even think I could."

He knelt down and wrapped his arms about her. "I'd do anything to change the last few days," he said.

"I know. Me too."

They both knew, of course, that this was impossible, that the joining was not, after all, to be a smooth melding together, but would be marked instead by a series of jagged edges that nicked, that cut, that left scabs.

"Do you still want to make love?" Amanda asked, wanting to, and wanting him to see her wanting to.

"I have a headache," Sam said.

She leaned back, looked at him.

"Oh what the hell," he said, smiling.

"Don't do me any favors."

"I'm not," he answered, messing her hair, pulling her up, kissing her. "You certainly didn't."

Amanda laughed for the first time in days.

Looking east, the skyline became abruptly lower, as if someone had taken a knife and quite deliberately pared away everything above five stories. There were no cranes here, heaving skyscrapers up out of the ground, no lipstick-shaped edifices to amuse or antagonize, there was no one arguing over shadows. Singed tenements sat like dominoes, occasionally splashed with colorful flowered curtains and men leaning out to chat with their friends on the street. In one of the vacant lots, the block association had planted a victory garden, and a few women and children stood bent over their plots, turning the soil for the winter.

A fleck of dust flew into Amanda's eye and she flinched but she didn't stop walking until she reached the corner of Barbara's block. She got out the scrap of paper she had written the phone number on and went into the *bodega* to let her know that she had arrived. Then she crossed the wide avenue, nodding to the mounted police, and stood before the scarred brownstone where Barbara was just now unlocking the front door. They kissed hello and Amanda followed her down a flight of poorly lit steps to the basement.

The warped wooden door swung open and they were slapped by a stream of harsh white lights pouring from the ceiling, Roxy Music blaring from the tiny speakers on the floor, and the work, on the walls, the tables, the floor, made, half-made, sketched, painted, enormous Plexiglas figures, their mammoth arms wrapped about each other, their large unfocused eyes looking not at each other but

179

out, at a spot just beyond, forever beyond the viewer, couples, families, holding onto each other in a futile attempt at comfort.

Amanda walked about the large studio in silence, aware of Barbara's eyes on her as she stopped before each piece.

"They're incredible," she said when she finally turned away from a particularly mournful group to Barbara. "You've changed so much since the last time I was here."

Barbara looked at her own creations for a minute, she was surprised by them too. "I know," she said, "but they're so much sadder. I've always done kind of cheerful work before. I wonder what people will think." She turned back to Amanda and removed the plastic goggles from the top of her head. A mass of brightly hennaed hair tumbled across her face and she brushed it impatiently aside.

"I think these are much more powerful," Amanda said tentatively, for she was wary of appearing to give any form of criticism.

"I think so too."

Amanda smiled, struck by the easy confidence with which Barbara accepted compliments as fact. She wondered if it was something that could be learned, or at least imitated.

"I started the series after I broke up with my boyfriend," Barbara said, smiling at herself.

"That'll do it."

"Yeah, well, he may be a shmuck but at least I got some good paintings out of it, right? Anyway, I heard you got married. That seems to be the fashionable thing to do these days. Sam Chapman, right? I remember seeing him around. I always thought he was a hot ticket."

Amanda smiled, but carefully. "I'll tell him you said so."

"So tell me, what's it like?"

"What?"

"Holy matrimony."

"It's good. It's different. I don't know, everything seems to take on more weight."

Barbara shrugged. "To tell you the truth, I don't think I'll ever get married. I seem to go in three-year cycles, never more, never less. I just think that's how it's always going to be."

"That seems kind of painful to me."

"Maybe. Anyway, tell me about your project." She poured some seltzer into plastic cups and wiped her hands on her faded orange overalls, parched, bitten, working hands. "I didn't quite get it when you called."

Amanda sat down on the floor, got out her notebook, empty save for a few aimless doodles, and began to go over the bare details. "I thought since you do so much three-dimensional work," she said, finishing up, smiling nervously—she had always been vaguely intimidated by Barbara, by her unabashed confidence and her ambition and even her three-year cycles—"well, I thought you might be interested."

"But what kind of jewelry do you mean exactly?"

"Whatever you want. Like your cutouts, for instance. Maybe you could . . ." she stopped short. "Whatever you want," she repeated.

Barbara thought for a minute, unconsciously picking up one of Amanda's pens and drawing directly onto the gray floor. "I'd have to play around with it," she said, "do some sketches." She looked over at Amanda. "What about costs?"

"We'd pay for materials. Then we'd split the selling price with you, just like a gallery. The thing is, we want you to have fun with it. You know."

"Well, I do have a show coming up in three months and I'm pretty busy with that." She was still drawing on the floor.

"We could guarantee you lots of publicity," Amanda said. She had always made a point before not to promise things she could deliver, much less things she couldn't.

"Who else is doing it?"

Amanda named some of the more well-known people on her list, none of whom had confirmed.

Barbara put down her pen. "Maybe it would be fun. How about if I think about it and let you know in a couple of days?"

"That would be great."

"So," Barbara said, standing up, "I ran into your old friend Bill the other night."

"Oh?"

"What's the line on him?"

Amanda laughed. "You interested?"

"Maybe."

"He doesn't go in three-year cycles."

"Men can be made to do any number of things with a little handiwork."

Amanda smiled uneasily. "Underneath the mess, he's a good person."

"Oh please," Barbara rolled her eyes. "I'm too old to think I'm going to uncover a choirboy beneath the dissolution. I just want to know what my best approach is."

"Somehow I think you can figure that out all by yourself."

Barbara laughed. "Right. Anyway, I'll give you a call in a couple of days, okay?"

"That would be great."

They kissed good-bye and Amanda made her way quickly up the steps.

It was a society girl's first novel and already it was the talk of all the magazine editors and aging debutantes and aspiring WASPs. Patrick, whose sister had gone to dancing school with her, had snapped up the rights and was planning on printing excerpts in two upcoming issues of *Backlog*. "Our first foray into fiction," he proclaimed.

"I think we should keep it down to four hundred," he said as he began to work on the guest list for the party. "Metaphorically speaking, of course. I'll leave it to your discretion." He smiled the lazy sphinxlike smile of a tired model. "I'm sure you know what I mean."

"Only too well," Sam muttered.

"What?"

"Nothing."

Patrick shrugged. He had discovered how much easier it was to simply ignore his moody editor's rumblings—the work always got done anyway.

The invitations, imitation Tiffany's printed in acid green, had gone out two weeks ago and already strangers were calling Sam at home, begging to be included. More often than not, he said yes, it was easier, he didn't much care.

Now he hung up the phone on an old college roommate of the author's—I'm sure she meant to send me an invitation, it's just that I've been moving around so much lately, you know how it is, that she probably had a hard time tracking me down, everyone does, except of course the people you don't want to find you and they know your number before you do, right? anyway, I know she'd want me to be there—and walked back into the kitchen to see what all the noise was. He stood in the doorway and broke out laughing—Amanda was vacuuming the inside of the Mr. Coffee.

"Would you mind telling me what you're doing?" he asked.

She turned to him and smiled. "Just a little spring cleaning, dear."

"First of all, it's not spring."

"Well it feels like it."

"It does, doesn't it? But anyway, normal people do not vacuum the inside of coffee makers."

Amanda shrugged. "I poured some coffee beans down the water chute by mistake. What would you do?"

He was laughing still. "I don't know. It makes sense, I guess. In your kind of way."

"My kind of way?"

"Well you do have a unique approach to house-cleaning. Let's not forget about last week when you defrosted the freezer with a blow dryer."

"It worked, didn't it?"

"Yes."

"So?"

His eyes were glistening as he went up to kiss her.

"Anyway, I thought it was my unique approach you loved so much."

"Did I say that?"

"Don't you?"

"I do. C'mon," he said, taking the long vacuum nozzle out of her hand, "let's get out of here. It's beautiful outside, it must be seventy degrees. This could be the last good day."

Amanda laughed. "And it's your optimism I love so much."

Outside, the illuminated clock over the bank said that it was in fact seventy-five degrees. Sam and Amanda walked with their arms around each other's waists, just like any other couple, married couple, happily married, who can tell? The last fingerprints of summer poked through the autumn sky and they watched the kids who just yesterday had been bundled up in coats and mittens now daring the season in thin sweaters. He kissed her temple where the wind blew back her hair and she was suddenly warmer than the day itself.

"Where to?" Amanda asked.

"I don't care. Anyplace."

They headed uptown, to long streets of buffed and polished doorjambs, buffed and polished faces, it could have been any city in the world here, tasteful, filigreed, safe as a pastry shell. Sam pointed to a mannequin in the window of a new French designer's outpost, bald and thin and dressed only in wide leather belts.

"Maybe that's what I should send home for Christmas. What do you think?" He had that virgin's face, when any information, any news at all is welcomed, it was what she loved, it was what she missed, and she slowed her pace and kissed him, diving in and out of it, that cavernous delight of his.

"I think your mother would love it," she said. "How can you go wrong? I'm sure they're one-size-fits-all."

"They don't know my mother."

Past the darkened windows of expensive bistros now, and apothecaries with beveled glasses of potions in the windows, past bookstores that promised only foreign imprints and florists with exotic concoctions wandering out of crystal vases, he took it in, and she did too—vacationers, partners—they took it all in, the women with their tight little suits and their ironed faces and the men with their assured steps.

Sam smiled and glued his eyes onto a woman with a leopard skin hat and matching tights. "Maybe I'll invite her to the party," he said. Amanda smiled too, they were on vacation after all.

Eventually, they turned around and started downtown on a different street, a newer street, lined with high white buildings and restaurants that changed nationality once a month. They stopped for a moment by a tiny park pried into the middle of a block and watched the children playing old familiar games, their mothers and their nannies hovering in the background, rubbing their arms as they chatted—the sun was sinking and it was no longer all that warm.

"So kids play hopscotch here just like they do in the rest of the world," Sam remarked.

"What did you think they played?"

"I don't know, I just kind of figured they were too busy sharpening their nails to be bothered."

"I thought you liked living here."

"I do."

"Oh."

He put his arm around her and she put her arm around him and they both were suddenly tired by the late gray afternoon.

"I wonder what causes it," Sam said when they got home and settled into the living room with a glass of wine.

"Causes what?"

"Days like this. Like nature forgot herself. Don't you ever wonder?"

"No," Amanda answered honestly, "I don't." She took a sip of her wine and in the stillness of the room she watched it grow, the children sharpening their nails and the hardness that night that was not for her and the sentences that had fallen dead and stinking to the floor, they grew from nothingness at her feet. "Why can't you just accept that there are some mysteries that you'll never understand? Not everything has an answer, a reason. Not everything fits into one of your little boxes." As soon as it had left her, she regretted it, he hadn't seen it, after all, growing from nothingness at her feet.

But Sam didn't rise to meet her, not like that. "Is that what you think?" he asked quietly.

"No. I don't know. Sometimes."

"I don't think everything has an answer. God, no, I don't think that at all. But I don't see what's wrong with trying to understand certain things. Some analysis is good."

"So is some mystery."

He drank his wine. "You can't use mystery as an excuse for everything."

"What does that mean?"

"Nothing, I don't know."

"Maybe not. But you can't rationalize away every impulse, anything that doesn't make immediate sense, you'll wind up dead, frozen and dead. Like Bill's quote, one of the wretched ones who never was alive."

Sam frowned. "What does Bill have to do with this?"

"Nothing."

"Anyway, by saying everything is a mystery, don't you think you're relinquishing all responsibility?"

"No."

"Oh."

In the growing darkness of the room, they realized that they had misplaced it, whatever it was that they were talking about, were trying to talk about, it had gotten coated and caked, and they both decided at once not to go looking for it. They were on vacation after all.

When they smiled at each other next they were together again, trying to be, yes.

"Do you want to go to that party tonight?" Amanda asked.

"If you want to."

"Well, I kind of feel I should. There are some people I promised to see."

"Then we'll go."

"You don't have to come if you don't want to. I can go alone."

"I thought husbands and wives were supposed to go out together."

"We don't have to. Not all the time. It's okay to do some things separately. Don't you think?"

"I guess. But I happen to like being with you."

Amanda smiled. "I happen to like being with you too."

"I knew we had something in common."

She missed Nancy. Despite the fact that they were once again seeing each other almost every morning at the store, something had happened, something had vanished, and she missed it, missed her, her best friend. It wasn't just the time she was spending on the jewelry project or Nancy's baby, it wasn't being married, there was another presence, a wary politeness, where there had once been eddies of sarcasm, of support. It hadn't been pushed out by a single exchange, one event, but had gradually faded, flattened, resurrecting itself in unexpected welcome little flashes that only served to remind them of what was missing.

Amanda unzipped her new red leather jacket and hung it from the back of her chair. She piled her bags and her sketch pads on top of the desk and poured herself a cup of coffee. What was it she wanted to tell Nancy about? Not the curtain she had caught glimpses of, veiling Sam's eyes from her, not the wildness that she had begun to feel welling up within, that shapeless rebellion that she had come to fear in herself—she thought she had outgrown it, outsmarted it, she thought she had married it away—pushing her insides out, calling her to run with it, to run and to run . . . No, not even that. She only wanted to look at Nancy, to have them read each other's thoughts as they used to, and say, "Let's go out tonight. Let's go dancing, let's stand in the corner and make fun of everyone who is not us"—just that.

Deirdre finished with a customer she had been trying

to talk into a micro-miniskirt and walked back to Amanda's desk.

"Hi," she said tentatively.

"Hi." Amanda continued flipping through the mail. "Did Nancy already leave for the day?"

"No. She just went out to get some lunch. She'll be back soon."

"Oh."

Deirdre could see from where she was standing that the front of the store was still empty and she stayed put, her hands moving slowly up the edge of the desk.

"Are you okay?" Amanda asked finally, looking up and seeing that she was definitely not okay.

Deirdre started to cry.

"Hey, what is it?"

"I don't know. Everything," she stammered. "My landlord won't renew my lease and this guy last night, I don't know, he seemed so nice, he took me home and then he passed out on my couch, I didn't even think he was that drunk, and then this morning he didn't even remember my name, and I don't have enough money to move and my roommate does and . . ."

Amanda stood up, sat Deirdre down in her chair, looked at her helplessly. She had forgotten about the unholy alliances that landlords and boys in bars and roommates can form when you're twenty-one. "It'll be okay," she said lamely. "It'll work out. Somehow things have a way of doing that, of working out." But promising anything seemed a treacherous game. "By the way," she said tentatively, "you do use condoms, don't you?"

When Nancy walked into Legacies, she was unpleasantly surprised by two customers in the front with no one there to wait on them or even keep an eye on the register. She asked if she could help them, her coat still on, her shoulder bag dangling from the crook in her arm, but they said that they were just looking and left.

"What's going on back here? Why isn't there someone up front?'' she asked as she walked back into the office. She stopped when she saw Deirdre crying, Amanda kneeling beside her. "Did something happen?"

Deirdre wiped her eyes, smiled. "No. It's okay. Sorry. I'll just go fix my makeup and go back up front."

"What was that all about?" Nancy asked when she was out of earshot.

"Greed, amnesia, the usual."

Nancy nodded as if she understood. "Funny, she didn't say anything to me this morning."

"It's just because we're here together more."

"Sure. Anyway, I'm glad you finished with your rounds this morning. There was something I wanted to talk to you about."

"I hope it's not a problem. I seem to be having my share of them lately."

"What's wrong?"

"Nothing. Forget it."

Nancy looked up from the phone messages she had been flipping through. "Amanda, fess up."

"Maybe it really is nothing." She smiled but it only creased one side of her face. "I just don't think Sam likes me anymore."

Nancy laughed. "He doesn't want to be your best friend?"

"Exactly."

"Can you give me some data?"

"That's the problem, there is none. At least none that I can find. It's just that sometimes he seems to be in another part of town, you know? Like there are whole neighborhoods between us. And I don't know how to get there."

"Are you arguing?"

"No. You know us, we never really argue much. I don't know what it is." She looked around for it, for a color, a scent. "Sometimes when he smiles," she said, "it seems to come from the outside in, instead of the other way around."

191

"You mean it's forced?"

"No, I mean it's too easy, it's so easy it scares me."

"So what do you do?"

Amanda smiled. "What do I do? Lately what I want to do is go too fast, you know? just go faster, go anywhere, make him meet me, make him come." She shrugged. "Of course, that's the one thing guaranteed to freeze his feet to the ground."

Nancy scratched her head with the tip of her pencil for a moment. "Sounds like PMS to me," she said finally.

"Oh c'mon. That's bullshit."

She smiled. "Not you. Him. Both of you. PMS. Postmarital shock."

"You think?"

"Absolutely. All the symptoms are in place. Withdrawal, the shakes, unexplained moodiness, a general inclination to escape, PMS, that's my guess."

"So what's the prescription, Madame Medic."

"I only diagnose. I don't prescribe."

"Thanks a lot."

"Anytime."

Amanda went back to her sketch pads, pulling a few drawings out and entering them into the portfolio that was leaning up against a plant and Nancy made a couple of phone calls.

"Nancy?" she asked when the phone was in its cradle.

"Yes?"

"Do you want to go out tonight?"

Nancy laughed. "Huh?"

"Go out, remember. Cut loose. Shake a leg. Paint the town. Go out."

"I do vaguely remember." She shook her head. "No, I can't. I mean, what about the baby?"

"Jack can take care of Ben."

"He's got far too much work to do. They're going to court in two weeks."

"Oh."

"I'm sorry. But anyway, I might not know all the answers, but I do know that going out with me isn't going to solve your problems."

"I wasn't looking for a solution, I was looking for some fun. So listen, what was it you wanted to talk to me about anyway?"

"Oh that. I got a call from the accessories editor of *Vogue*. She wanted to know when our line was debuting. I thought it was time we set up some kind of schedule."

"There are still a lot of people's work I haven't even seen yet."

"Well I have to call her back and tell her something."

"Why don't you let me handle it?"

Nancy looked at her and shrugged. "Fine. But we still have to come up with a schedule."

"I know."

Glancing across the crowded gallery she spotted him leaning up against the thick cement pillar, his arms crossed, his face expressionless, and for an instant, he was a stern and authoritative figure to her, he was all the chaperones at all the high school dances—benign, observant, resented. Amanda straightened her back and made her eyes shine high for the man she was talking to, as if their artificial light would fall on Sam, as he leaned up against the pillar, his arms crossed. She broadened her smile till it hurt.

"So what's your excuse for being here tonight?" Bill asked.

"Do I need one?"

"No one needs one, but everyone always seems to have one."

"I told you about the project I'm trying to put together for Legacies. There are some people coming I want to see."

"Raping artists' notebooks?"

"It's not as much fun as raping artists, but it's a start."

"Your husband looks like he's having a great time."

They both glanced over at Sam, who was looking elsewhere, at a woman with lilac speckles in her hair. Amanda turned back to Bill. "Doesn't he though?"

"Is everything okay?"

"Groovy."

Bill laughed.

"It doesn't matter," she said. "I'd rather talk to you. It's been far too long."

"Through no fault of mine."

"Oh c'mon. You're the San Andreas of boyfriends."

"How would you know?"

"What do you mean, how would I know? We have crossed paths every now and then."

"But I was never your boyfriend."

"No, of course not. We didn't believe in all those mundane things, possession, stability . . ."

"Continuity," Bill added, "accountability . . ."

"Not us."

"Not me."

"Ah for the good old days of carefree selfish lust. Gone with all those other dreams."

Bill laughed. "So does this mean you won't be coming to the restaurant later?"

"We'll be there."

"That's what I always loved about you. No distraction was too small to get you out."

"Out of what?"

"That's your problem, don't you think?"

Amanda frowned. "Christ, Bill, I hate it when you do that."

"Do what?"

"Pretend to know more about me than you do."

"Are you so sure I don't?"

"All I know is that I have no more sympathy for the devil."

Bill smiled. "I'll see you later."

There were thirty of them, the artist and her friends and other guests of the gallery owner, spread down the back of the restaurant in two long rows. Amanda sat between Sam, his stony smile, his silence—she couldn't remember the last time she had heard his voice—and Bill, with his secret tombstone eyes, she sat between them in her new red silk cocktail dress cut so low that when she leaned to one or the other, her chest was almost bared, she wanted it that way, why not? there was a hard power in attraction and she armed herself with it gladly, defiantly, raising it higher and testing its strength as a weapon, as a shield, it was hers, why not? She finished her first glass of wine before the waiter had distributed the rest of the round and quickly ordered another. Sam was resolutely looking elsewhere.

"So," Amanda said loudly, turning to Bill, "I finally went to that fortune teller you told me about."

Bill laughed. "That was two years ago."

"What difference does it make? I thought you believed in parallel time."

Sam wasn't listening. Her dress slipped off of her shoulder and she left it there but he wasn't watching either.

"Are you going to tell me what the lady said?" Bill asked.

"She said I should stay away from doctors."

"What does that mean? Have you been sick?"

"Sick? No. Not that I know of, anyway. She looked at both of my palms, what is it? intention and actuality, and she said that I would have many near nervous breakdowns in my life but I would always get over them by myself unless I went to a doctor and then . . . "

"Then?"

She smiled, shrugged, she couldn't tell if Sam was listening or not. "Then I would melt like the Wicked Witch of the West."

Bill smiled and pulled her dress back onto her shoulder. "I don't think they use water treatments anymore. Intention and actuality, huh?"

Amanda nodded. "All engraved by the gods right into your skin."

"And which would you rather have?"

Sam had turned completely around now, to the woman on his right, a lawyer in an expensive suit who was discussing the recent Supreme Court ruling on privacy, he was watching her, watching the words sputter from her expensive mouth, but all he heard was the sound of Amanda's dress slipping from her shoulder and being lifted back, intention and actuality, he didn't care, not really, not tonight, for tonight she seemed to have nothing to do with him, tonight she was leaning further and further out, with her game-show sociability and her cocktail party mysticism, out into the lights and the din that had once fascinated him and tonight seemed only like a spinning crystal ball on an empty dance floor, dizzying and pointless and sad.

"I don't suppose I could have them both?" Amanda asked.

"Don't ask me, ask the gypsy, ask your husband."

"But I'm asking you."

Bill smiled. "On good nights. On good nights, for a minute or two, you can have them both."

Amanda smiled too. "On good nights."

He was eating now, his Cajun shrimp, eating carefully, neatly avoiding the shells, and she turned and smiled at him as the fork fell from his mouth, she turned and smiled with all the souped-up voltage of a cityful of manic nights, and he smiled back, his mouth closed, battened down, he had to protect himself from the glare, and that was how they were caught when, for just an instant, they simply scared each other. They both backed up and blinked.

"How is it?" Amanda asked.

"What?"

"The shrimp."

"It's fine. You want to taste it?"

"No. That's okay."

Sam returned to his plate, to the lawyer who sat waiting impatiently for his easy attention, and Amanda turned once more to Bill, but she found Barbara standing between them, playing with his tie.

"I've been meaning to call you for weeks," she was saying.

"I've been hoping you would."

"Then should I?"

"Will you still respect me in the morning?"

"I don't respect you now."

"Good," Bill said, "it's the perfect basis to start with. Don't you think, Amanda?"

She nodded and turned back to her own plate.

Sam and Amanda were among the last to leave, staying seated as people up and down the aisles gradually drifted off, until only a handful of people were left, moving one by one to the center of the long table, twined together by a reticence to say it was enough, to say it was over, all of them squeezing and squeezing the night until they were certain it was dry and then squeezing it more. Sam tapped his foot under the table while Amanda reminisced about a party long ago, when they had been younger, when they knew how to have a good time, when penalties were years away and no one had heard of petrified forests. Her hair was in her eyes and she left it there, it felt okay, it felt good, why not? she drank a brandy to keep the light from fading. ". . . that was the time I locked myself in my bedroom by mistake," she was saying, ". . . when the police had to come to get me out, remember that," she was saying, ". . . that was when we drove Peter's heap up Madison Avenue until it stalled and we left it there . . ." she was saying, "remember that?"

Sam turned to her. "I have to get up early in the morning," he said.

She looked at him for a moment and then she finished her brandy in one gulp. "Fine."

In the cab, she propped her long legs through the glass partition so that her red high heels were next to the driver's face and he turned around and growled, "Do you mind?"

She shrugged and pulled her legs back in.

"What's with you tonight?" Sam asked.

"What's with me? What the hell is wrong with you? You've been scowling at me since we left the apartment. Why didn't you just tell me if you didn't want to go?"

"I didn't say I didn't want to go."

"You didn't say anything. All you do is stand there and look disapproving."

"That's ridiculous. Disapprove of what?"

"You tell me."

"I just see no reason that we had to stay so late."

"No?"

"No."

The cab was stuck behind a garbage truck that was slowly clearing the street of its bagged-up trash and they paused while the two drivers yelled at each other in Spanish and the car horns went off and on and off.

"We'll get out here," Sam said, and he pushed some bills into the slot.

Amanda climbed out and fell automatically into her rapid hop hop hopping walk but it wasn't what she meant and she forced herself to slow down, she had only wanted to reach him after all. "I only wanted to have a good time," she said.

"And did you?"

"No."

They had reached the front door and Sam fumbled with the keys.

"Me neither," he said.

They walked up the stairs in silence and Amanda took her earrings off as they climbed.

"Sam?" she said when they got inside. "How could I have a good time when you were so far away?"

He hung up his coat, brushed back his hair. "You weren't exactly within arm's reach either."

They walked back into the bedroom but they waited to undress.

"I don't know," Sam said. "I guess I'm just tired tonight. Maybe I should have stayed home."

"Is that all it is?"

He reached over and touched her face with his calloused fingertips. "Sure," he said, "that's all it is," and they kissed standing up, their clothes still on.

In the night, she felt the burden of desire shift, settle down on her like a cloud, a dense fog.

He lay still beside her, his steady even breathing like a steel gate, barring her entrance. He had kissed her good night, he had called her honey, he had done nothing wrong, nothing at all, except the way he had crossed his arms, the way he had left her here, outside, alone, and that was nothing at all, not really. She looked at his placid face, his thin motionless lids shut over his eyes, he was just tired, that was all, eyes that had been looking beyond her all night, leaving her outside, alone, with no explanation, with nothing but the ephemeral power of defiance. It seemed impossible to move him.

Amanda slid carefully out of the bed and went into the living room. She poured herself a brandy and sat on the floor warming it between her hands and she was where she had been so many times before, in the middle of the lost hours, sore from having danced too fast, trying to outdance it, all the inevitabilities that grew in the night, the lost hours that his touch had not erased, not eradicated after all, had he promised that they would? she couldn't remember, the alone lost hours that he had closed his arms against, and suddenly all she thought she had found twisted into all she would never be able to hold. Downstairs, she could hear a television endlessly blaring the news. He had slipped away when she wasn't looking.

She took a sip of her brandy and watched the shadows that the street lights made flickering across her legs like pale white dancers, ghosts of good times gone—he had done nothing wrong, nothing at all. He had only gone to sleep, gone and taken it with him, the promise of him, the promise to eradicate the lost hours, taken it with him when he stood across the gallery, leaning up against the pillar, his arms crossed, taken it with him when he scowled in the cab, taken it with him when he watched her like a chaperone and when he disappeared for hours, and he had taken it with him when he kissed her with cold closed lips. She finished her brandy in one hard long biting gulp and poured herself another—he had done nothing wrong, nothing at all, he was just tired, that was all. He was, as usual, above reproach. Someone had turned the television off and the room was suddenly quiet as a coffin and it scared her. She took her snifter into the bathroom and drew herself a hot bath, crawling into its warmth like a weary diver, the warmth that warmed for an instant but had to be left behind.

Amanda walked on soft wet feet into the bedroom and stood in the doorway watching him sleep so calmly without her—as if he had done nothing wrong. Clean and warm and naked, she went to his desk, pausing for a moment, yes, she paused, paused before the orderly surface of it, and then, slow and quiet, she slid open the cabinet drawer, the one he kept so tightly shut, she slid it open, slid it toward her, perhaps there?—but the sound of it reached him, reached him someplace, wherever he was without her, and he groaned and rolled over in his sleep. She shut the drawer and went to the bed, climbing in beside him and settling one arm across the expanse of his broad back.

"You okay?" he mumbled sleepily.

"Yes. Just a little restless."

He moved just enough to pat her behind and then he pulled his arm back to his side and she was left where she had started, lonelier than all the lost hours alone on the living room floor, lonelier than that, as she listened to his steady even sleep breathing beside her.

In the morning, he rolled on top of her. He brushed his lips skittishly across her cheek and she wrapped her arms about his back—at last. His hand slid over her small breasts and they rose to meet it and then it traveled down her waist and her hips and in between her legs and he came upon a tampon string. He rolled over onto his back without saying a word and they lay like that, parallel, still.

"I got my period," Amanda said finally.

"So I see."

They were touching only where they had to.

"It's not contagious," she said.

"I know." He paused. "Well why don't you take the damn thing out?"

She pulled out the tampon and dropped it on the floor beside the bed—for even when she didn't want him, she wanted him. They made love quickly and then they went to work.

Lucy crossed her legs so that her snug denim dress rose high above her shapely knees. Her hair was pulled into a loose cascading ponytail on the side of her head and calculated strands washed across her cheek. "I couldn't help but watch your wife at dinner last night," she said to Sam. "She seemed to be having such a good time."

Sam unsnapped his eyes from her legs. "She likes parties."

When she cocked her head, her eyebrows seemed to form a pornographic question mark. "Do you?"

He looked at her, at the challenge and the will, at the dark lashes that fringed her almond eyes—but it wasn't what he wanted. That much, at least, he knew. "I like her," he said.

Lucy smiled. "Well I should hope so." And then she slid off of the desk and walked away, with her cameras and her film, with her open invitation, and Sam went back to what he was doing, compiling a list of most unlikely couples for February's Valentine issue.

When he left the office an hour later, a wet rainy snow was dripping down and he turned up his collar and walked quickly, but even then, he couldn't force himself down into the subways. He stepped from the curb and began to walk in the street, his eyes up, his hands out, futilely searching for a cab, he wanted only to be home, it wasn't the cold or the wet, he wanted only to be home, he would take her in his arms, he would tell her he was sorry, about last night, about this morning, he would tell her that. He had walked all but the last three blocks when a cab stopped before him. "Never mind," he told the driver.

Amanda hadn't gotten home yet and Sam hung up his damp overcoat and shook a few wet droplets from his hair before going over to the blinking red light and listening to the afternoon's messages, theirs, his, hers. His throat clutched at the fifth one, but he knew what to do, breathe evenly, concentrate, regulate, it was a trick he had learned long ago, it was what one had to do, breathe evenly, concentrate, regulate. He rewound the tape so that it would be ready for her and then he went into the kitchen and waited.

Sam was staring into the sink when Amanda finally came in.

"Hi?" she asked as the door closed behind her.

"Hi."

She hung up her coat and went to kiss him hello and he let her do it before he said anything. "Amanda?"

"Yes?"

"Would you mind telling me why there are paper clips in the sink?"

She laughed and shrugged and started to walk away. "Well?"

"How should I know?"

He continued to remove a pile of scummy plates and cups that rose to precarious heights, he tried to do it, to breathe evenly, carefully, even when one of the glasses slipped from his wet hands and crashed to the floor—they had lost control of the apartment.

Sam followed Amanda into the living room where she was sitting on the couch and glancing through the Christmas catalog from the Metropolitan Museum.

"Look," he said, "we can't go on like this."

She looked up from the copper angels, relieved. "No," she said softly. "We can't."

"There's no reason for it."

"I feel the same way."

"Then let's set up a cleaning schedule."

"A cleaning schedule? Is that what you're talking about?"

"Of course. What are you talking about?"

"Us."

"Us?"

"Yes. Us." She closed the catalog and dropped it on the ground and she tried to smile. "Don't you think things have been a little out of whack lately?"

What had he meant to do, tell her he was sorry, about last night, about this morning, tell her that? "What do you mean, out of whack?" he asked.

"How can you be so eagle-eyed about a little dust and so blind about us?"

"A little dust? This place is disgusting. I don't know how you can stand living like this."

"Fine. If that's all that's bothering you, we'll get a housekeeper."

"We can't afford a housekeeper." This wasn't it, this wasn't it at all, he didn't know what it was.

"We can afford someone one day a week."

"No we can't. Besides, it's a waste of money. If you would just try to be a little neater . . ."

"I have no intention of turning into a household drudge."

"I hardly think doing the dishes occasionally or picking up your clothes constitutes severe hardship."

Amanda said nothing. This wasn't it, this wasn't it at all, she didn't know what it was.

"And I also don't think it would kill us to stay home and cook dinner once in a while."

"Anything else? Any goddam thing else?"

"I'm sorry," Sam said. "I just think it's time we settled down a little."

"Settled down? What's that supposed to mean? Just

because we're married doesn't mean we have to start going around in wheelchairs."

"This is ridiculous," Sam said. "Just forget it. Forget the whole damn thing. I'm going in to take a shower."

"Suit yourself."

He began to walk past her down the hallway. "By the way," he said, turning partially around, breathe evenly, concentrate, regulate, "there were some messages for you on the machine."

Amanda waited until she could hear the water going full blast before pressing the on button. A hang-up, someone inviting them to a party, Nancy asking where the invoice was for the wrap-around sweaters, Bill wanting to discuss Barbara, Barbara wanting to discuss Bill, and a voice more familiar than her own, Tom. He just wanted to say hello, he would love to see her, lunch? dinner? breakfast? he missed her, remember? He left a number. Amanda listened to it twice and then she erased it, certain that the number was unlisted, irretrievable. She didn't want to be tempted.

When Sam finally came out of the bathroom he went into the bedroom and sat down on the bed where Amanda was studiously watching television. She moved over just enough to make room for him and kept her eyes on the screen and he followed them and watched along with her for a few minutes. "What's happening?" he asked. It seemed to be a sitcom.

"It's too complicated to explain."

"Oh."

They watched in silence until a commercial for a domestic airline came on.

"Sam?" Amanda continued to watch a plane soaring through a bluer than blue sky.

"Yes?"

"I didn't ask him to call. It's not my fault. I mean, I haven't talked to him since that time we ran into him on the street."

"Oh."

They watched the plane land, they listened to a bunch of raisins singing, the sitcom returned.

"Anyway, it's not that," she went on. "And I know it's not just the paper clips in the sink either. So what are you so upset about?"

"What makes you think I'm so upset?"

"Oh please."

"I don't know what it is."

"Well just for the record, I don't want to be with anyone else," Amanda said. "I want to make this work."

"I know. So do I."

The next hour's show came on, undercover cops, something like that.

"So?"

"I don't know," Sam said, his curl between his fingers. "I guess I just thought it would different, easier."

"What would be easier?"

"Us. Marriage."

"You didn't really think we'd wake up one day and be Ozzie and Harriet, did you?"

Sam smiled. "Maybe."

There was synthesizer music, bullet shots, opening credits.

"You mean you thought we'd magically turn into these other people, these nice simple full-of-answers people the minute we got married?"

"Didn't you?"

Amanda shrugged. "Lately I feel like I lost track of the question." She moistened her lips, she still didn't look at him. "Sam? Where do you go?"

"What do you mean?"

"I'm not sure what I mean. I just know you go someplace and leave me behind."

"So do you."

"That doesn't answer my question."

The woman with the blue heels, the notebooks and the walls. "I don't go anyplace," he said. "I'm here."

They watched as the cops moved in on an oily teenage boy with pants so tight he had to be trouble.

"Oh."

"Sometimes you seem very distant to me too," he said.

"What is it I do that makes me feel distant?"

"Running in place."

"Maybe I'm just trying to catch up with you."

"It feels more like you're trying to escape me."

"I don't want to," she said. She turned and put her

hand on his knee and looked at him for the first time. "That's the last thing in the world I want." He touched her too.

"I'm sorry about last night," he said. "I'm sorry about this morning. I'm sorry about this evening."

Amanda smiled. "That's a lot of sorry's. I'm sorry too."

"For what?"

"For whatever it is that makes us go away from each other."

"What about what makes us come back?"

"I'm not sorry for that."

"No, me neither."

"No?"

"No. So," Sam said, smiling sheepishly, "do you want to go out to dinner?"

Amanda laughed. "You sure you don't want me to fix you something? Meat loaf? Mashed potatoes? Jello mold?"

Sam rolled his eyes. "I didn't marry you for your cooking skills."

"'Why did you marry me?"

"Because for some idiotic reason I happen to be in love with you."

"Idiotic?"

"Okay, brilliant. Brilliant reasoning told me you were the one for me."

Amanda smiled. "Let's not push the issue."

"Now where do you want to go for dinner?"

"Sam?"

"Yes?"

"I'm in love with you too."

They were too close to kiss and they stood up instead.

"Mexican?" Sam asked.

They walked to the restaurant hand in hand and they talked and laughed about little things, things that had nothing to do with them, things that went away.

PART FOUR

It was gray and gray again, it was a month designed for brooding. Already, February seemed bottomless, endless. Sam and Amanda found themselves in more and more unlikely places, out-of-the-way bars, unpopular restaurants, cabarets where they were certain not to run into anyone they knew, anything too familiar.

Often, they went as high as they could, seated across from each other at tables in various rooftop venues dotted like a string of lights across the city's ceiling, as if they thought they could find what they had misplaced by looking down upon it. At least from there the streets appeared to have some order, some plan. You never knew then, when you would glance down, or perhaps out, past the city's perimeters—it is finite, after all—and find it. These bars thrust into penthouse towers that others saved for special occasions, expense accounts, tourist trips, became their comfort, their refuge.

"Maybe northern California," Amanda said desultorily. Lately, they had gotten into the habit of waking each other up with some new location, different climate, and then looking over as if waiting for a bell to go off—jackpot! But neither really believed it was anything more than a game, though at times they pretended otherwise.

Sam nodded, he was hardly listening. He continued to push the salted honey nuts around in their little crystal bowl, and Amanda returned to the window, to the dirty slush piled on the streets far below.

"I spoke to Mark this morning," Sam said, picking up

a nut, putting it carefully down. His voice was studied, slow, removed.

"Oh?" She returned to him. "How is he?"

"Good. It looks like the backing for the film came through."

"That's terrific."

"Yeah."

She took a couple of the nuts, unconsciously destroying the pattern he had created. "Are you jealous?" she asked.

"Of Mark? No."

"Well you don't exactly sound pleased for him either. Second thoughts?"

"No, I had no choice. I couldn't have done it then."

"Of course you had a choice. Free will, remember."

"We hardly made it through the holidays with the shirts on our backs. How would it have been if I hadn't had a paycheck coming in?"

"We would have made it somehow. The question is, how would you be now? Happier?"

"Somehow." Sam smiled and shook his head. "Happier? I don't know. Maybe."

They looked across the small table at each other and each took a sip of their drinks simultaneously. A few feet away, a group of men in three-piece suits were toasting someone's promotion.

"Too many earthquakes in California," Sam said. "How about the south? Atlanta? New Orleans?"

"Maybe."

The dinner crowd was beginning to enter and it was time for them to leave. "Ready?" Sam asked.

Amanda nodded.

They smiled at each other in the elevator as their ears popped and he put his arm around her waist, they were still in it together at least.

Outside, they walked on paths shoveled through the discolored snow, sometimes side by side, sometimes in single file. Despite the dampness, the cold, it was good to be outside, to be moving, even if slowly. All down the street, Final Sale signs were promising unbelievable bargains and they waited patiently for each other when something in a window caught one or the other's eye. Sam peered into a sports shop's display of running shoes, marked down forty percent, shrugged, and began walking again.

They came next to a row of restaurants and night clubs, black and brightened boxes of light, of warmth. As they passed a singles' bar someone was just leaving and a heady gust of rock 'n' roll poured out of the open door and into the street. Both looked in at once, glimpsing only darkness, averted faces.

Amanda smiled. "Do you think there are postseason sales on romance too?"

Sam laughed. "God, I feel so old."

The music tried to follow them, but it faded a little with every step.

"You're only thirty-one," she said quietly. "You're so young."

In fact, neither of them had ever felt quite young and it seemed too late to start now.

They could no longer hear the music at all.

"My toes are numb," Amanda said. "Let's get a cab."

"Okay."

"New Orleans is too humid," Amanda called to Sam as he stood in the middle of the street, staring down the oncoming traffic in search of a taxi. "How about Cape Cod?"

Sam finally got one, held the door open for Amanda to slide in, then climbed in after her, shut the door, and gave the driver their address. "A little house on the beach," he said. "No neighbors at all except in the summer. The quiet life, that's the life for us . . ."

They both laughed and he rested his hand on her knee.

This time, it was a man.

What was he wearing?
A navy suit, well-made from the slices of it Sam could
see, a Burberry overcoat open to show the orange and
brown plaid, a face that the world had promised a tan,
and given, given that and more, the steadfast features and
the rectangular chin with just the shadow of a jowl that
would not fully appear for years, until it was needed, the
up-ahead eyes—he was a metal splinter from another
structure, he was everything Sam would never be, everything he despised, with his place in the world that fitted
and fitted and had never done anything else, no, surely
not, he thought, never a curve, never a pockmark, he
thought as he followed, he just fitted and fitted . . .

This time, it was easier. He had spotted him a few
yards ahead and it was as obvious as a magnet, they
were walking in the same direction, why not then? it was
easier, it was clearer than going home, easier than turning
away, the overcoat barely creased with the man's long
strides, never a curve, never a pockmark, surely not, Sam
watched the back of his head, his blond hair just beginning to fade, and he knew now that it wasn't a woman
after all, not a woman at all, it was a different kind of
research he was doing, never a curve, never a pockmark,
surely his eyes had never fastened on the ground, not
him, not this man the world had promised so much to and
given, Sam felt the instantaneous hatred and respect of the
hunter for his prey, he turned right at the corner and Sam
followed, followed the man with the paper folded in

quarters beneath his arm and a wedding band on his hand, followed and wondered what she was like, if she wore perfectly cut clothes too and if he missed her during the day, or at night, did he miss her even when he held her tight, did she fit and fit too or did she only want to go out dancing all night like a scared little Sufi, he wondered what they argued about, this man with the paper and the wedding band and the tan who never fastened his eyes to the ground but trusted his feet to know where to fall, always to know, was it about mortgages and nursery schools, about balancing the checkbook and bills from Bendel's, is that what couples, couples like them, argued about? The man shifted his brown attaché case from his left hand to his right without disturbing his stride, they didn't argue, he and Amanda, not now, not really, and they certainly didn't have mortgages and children and unbalanced checkbooks, all they had was a sad sagging gray distance, the man's pants had a perfect cuff kissing the top of his oxford shoes and Sam wondered if he had a perfect cuff kissing the top of oxford shoes and a paper folded in quarters beneath his arm if he would fit and fit and all the sad sagging gray distance would wash away like the dunes, the man wove through a group of women coming in the opposite direction without looking at their faces and Sam hurriedly threaded through their lineup, he wanted to cut him up, this man with the up-ahead eyes and the promised face, he wanted to cut him up and see if he bled, if he scared, if he scarred, he waited a few feet away for the light to change and then crossed the congested avenue behind him, he wanted to go up with his notebooks and his pens and ask him if there were curvatures hidden beneath the overcoat and the suit, if there were pockmarks, ask him if it ever terri-fied him to lie in bed at night and watch it, watch each piece falling in and in and into place, the next one and the next, an endless wall of pieces, fitting in night after night after night, a lifetime of pieces, a lifetime of nights behind and ahead until it seemed that there would never be anything else, he wanted to go up with his notebooks and his pens and ask him if his feet ever itched to kick it all away, kick it to the stars, it wasn't what he had meant after all, kick it until even the dusty jigsaw outline of the pieces fitting one by one by one was gone and it was empty again, did he ever want to do that? this man with the perfect cuff and the oxford shoes and the fading hair, did he ever want to wipe it all away with one swift move of his well-toned arm, he was heading into an Italian gourmet shop now, crammed with early evening shoppers, and Sam let the door close fully before reopening it and following him in, into the yellow-lit wooden room stuffed with hanging baskets of meats and breads, rows of dark oily coffee beans in polished glass cases and counters of cheeses and spreads in pale whites and yellows and oranges, what was he buying? Sam leaned forward, straining to hear, there were three people on line between them, a pound and a half of smoked mozzarella, a tin of pitted black olives, it was Sam's turn and he bought a loaf of bread and followed him to the next line by the register, absently fingering the heel of the loaf, until the man with the rectangular chin and the wife and the paper folded in quarters beneath his arm turned suddenly around and asked in an unlikely high voice, "Do I know you?" and Sam had to say, "No." Outside, they went in opposite directions.

Sam decided to stop for a beer before going home—it didn't make much difference, Amanda wouldn't be there yet anyway, she'd been working late almost every night for the past two weeks, so many loose ends, so many things to tie up before the unveiling, so much to do, things only I can do, really—and he went into a worn-down old bar with grimy green and gold lettering across the chipped marquee, a neglected bar where he could slink down into a low greasy little table in a corner by himself and wait until the heat in his cheeks—caught,

caught me, he caught me, he knew—could hit up against the cold beer and subside, subside into the darkness and the sour smell rising from the planked floor and the timeless brown air, wait until a colder calm pulled up within, and then he dug out his notebook and he tried to brush away a few of the table's stains before he spread open its pages and began to write, "This time, it was a man . . ."

A long slab of plywood took up most of the front half of the loft and they sat at the end of it on high bar stools, they had been sitting there for over an hour with the drawings opened up one by one and the thin wall of country music that barely covered up the gurgles of Chinatown below them and the improbable lace curtains that now had the dusk filling up their delicate nettings. He had faded white paint in his hair and speckled onto his jeans like melted snow and by now she had wanted to take it between her fingers and brush it away, for how long? long enough to know she was in trouble. His royal blue turtleneck was worn softer than . . . she took a swallow of her wine.

"So with all this chitchat about proportions and proposals, you haven't even told me how your holidays were," Neil said.

"God, it seems like so long ago. They were okay. How about you?"

"They sucked."

Amanda laughed. "Mine too."

He had carbonated eyes and a slightly crooked smile. "What happened?"

"Nothing. I don't know." She smiled down at his knees curving against his jeans, ran her finger round and round the lip of her wine glass. "My husband seems to be going through some sort of a mid-life crisis."

"I didn't know you married an older man."

"Neither did I."

"Huh?"

She smiled but a waft of disloyalty was seeping in beneath the door and she wrinkled her nose—anyway, she didn't particularly want Sam in the room right now. "What went wrong with you?"

"Oh just your basic holiday wreckage. My girlfriend had a major nervous breakdown on New Year's Eve and spent the whole night rambling on about biological clocks. It seems her resolution was that if I don't marry her within six months it's time for me to hit the road."

"And what was your resolution?"

"My resolution was to wait five months and twenty-nine days and then flip a coin. No. I don't know."

There was only an inch left in the bottle and Neil reached over and divided it between their glasses. "What about you?" he asked as he rested the bottle on its belly and twirled it in a circle, round and round and slowly round. "Are you planning on having children?"

She watched it go, the neck, the body, the neck, round and round. "Not this month."

Neil laughed. "Talk about your loaded subjects. I'm sorry, I guess it's just on my mind lately. Anyway, there's something I didn't show you. Now that I know you like the sketches, I have a surprise for you."

"Oh?"

"I made up a pair of earrings for you. I know I was supposed to wait, but I really wanted to see what they looked like." He smiled indulgently at his own enthusiasm as if it were a minor bad habit that he couldn't quite control.

Amanda smiled too and let it fall, the cloak that she had lately felt obligated to drape over her own enthusiasm as if it were a bad accent that might offend Sam, she let it slide to the floor and when she rose, she was wonderfully light and mobile. "C'mon," she said as she pulled Neil off of his stool too, "show me."

He laughed and walked quickly over to the cluttered

drafting table near the window, pushing aside a pyramid of pens and chalks and boxes and bills and dug out a pair of freshly soldered earrings. He did not hold them out to her but put his arms about her waist and led her to a dusty full-length mirror propped up against a stack of records. He stepped behind her, his stomach pressing up against her back, close, touching, and held them to her ears, his breath close and touching too. The earrings were delightful thin wire figures with dangling copper balls that swung this way and that and their childish sweetness made Amanda laugh as they dipped about her neck.

"I love them," she said, looking at the reflection of his eyes, auburn, they were auburn, in the mirror.

"Good." He let the cold metal tickle her neck and suddenly she wasn't laughing anymore, there was the cold metal and the warmth of his breath, there was the white paint in his hair that she only wanted to rub between her fingers, he was easy as molasses, this one, he was nothing but easy, this one, as he touched her lightly on the waist and turned her to him like a puppet, close, touching, with his auburn eyes sliding into hers. Sam's desire for her had lately felt more like an experiment than desire and she had forgotten anything else, forgotten this. She took it between her fingers, the strand of hair with its melted snow, she had to give herself that much at least. It wasn't easy at all. "I can't," she said.

His hands stayed on the small of her back. "I know," he said gently. "I can't either."

It rubbed her open—I can't either—it roughed her up, it was easy and hard and inevitable and Sam had never been in a room as much as he was in this one. "I should get going," she said, still in his arms. Still in his eyes. "I, I have a lot to do tonight if I'm going to fit these pieces into the collection."

"I know. And I really am glad you're going to include them. Here," he said, taking the earrings that had somehow landed in her hands, he let his fingers touch her palms slow and smooth, he wasn't embarrassed or sorry and neither was she, "here, let me wrap them up for you."

She watched as he put the earrings on a large thick piece of drawing paper and then carefully folded it in and out and in until he handed it back to her, a perfect swan.

She smiled. "How did you do that?"

"Just one of my talents."

"I wish . . ."

He smiled too. "So do I."

And then he put the earrings in her coat pocket and kissed her good-bye.

She could hear it even before she was fully inside of
the front door, his voice talking rapidly into the empty
room, "Amanda, are you there? I know you're there,
playing hide and seek, hiding, I can always tell when
you're there, and I know you're there, so just come on
over and pick up the phone, you can do it, I want to talk
to you, want to talk, c'mon, darling, I know you're home,
it's your father, here, come, all you have to do is just walk
to . . ."

She dropped her portfolio on the floor and walked
over to the machine. "Dad?"

He erupted into a loud satisfied laugh. "I knew it. I
have a sixth, or is it a fifth, well whatever sense it is, I
have it, always did when it comes to you, you know that,
now listen darling . . ."

"Where are you, Dad?"

"Where am I? I'm home."

"You're not home. I can hear all those noises. It
sounds an awful lot like a bar to me."

"Home, New York. New York is home. Always has
been. Not Connecticut, not ever really Connecticut, what
a place, all green and dead, she was so good about it too,
so good it . . ."

"Why are you calling me?"

"What's the matter? Don't you like talking to me? I
always like talking to you. I have something I want to talk
to you about. Serious. Don't you want to talk to me? I
need to, I told you, I need to talk to you, darling. Con-

224

necticut, old and green and dead Connecticut, with all those houses full of good women. Well, I'm home now. Home."

"Okay, you're home. But where are you really? I mean, right now? Where?"

"Upper East Side. Don't know. Fifty-seventh, Fifty-eighth. I wanted to talk to you before I go back to see your mother. Maybe Fifty-ninth."

"Don't."

"Don't what?"

"Please, Dad. Don't go see Mom like this."

"Like what?"

"Talk to me first. You said you wanted to talk to me, something serious. Tell me where you are and I'll come get you."

His laughter rumbled into the phone for a minute. "Remember that time I had to come get you at the airport, where were you coming home from, darling? always so stubborn and silent, and so poor you didn't have the fare back into town. What a lost little teenager you were."

"Dad, ask someone the address."

"Want to talk to your mother. That's what I want to do. I want to talk to you first, then your mother. Home. It's good to be home. Isn't that a song? It must be." She lost him to a little harmony with the words home and home again crackling in and out. "Fifty-sixth and First," he said, coming back. "Restaurant in the middle of the block. Come meet me and I'll buy you dinner. Your sister too. Why not let the old man treat his two girls to dinner? And your mother too. I'll call her next, my three favorite women in the world, that's what I'll do, I'll call . . ."

"No, Dad. Why not let it be just the two of us? We never get a chance to talk alone anymore. Wouldn't it be nice? Just the two of us? Okay?"

"Sure, darling, whatever you want. Fifty-sixth and First. Restaurant in the middle of the block."

"Promise me something?"

"Anything, anything at all. You know that."

"Stay put, okay? Just stay there and don't call anyone else. It'll be our secret. I'll hop in a cab and be there in fifteen minutes. Just stay right where you are. Okay?"

"Of course. You think I'm drunk. I can tell that's what you think. But I'm not. One or two. But not drunk."

"Okay. I'll be there in ten minutes."

"I thought you said fifteen?"

"I'm leaving right now, Dad. Go back and sit down and wait for me."

"Of course."

Mr. Easton's elbows were sunk into the bar like quicksand but his navy blazer wasn't the least bit askew. His reddened neck rose from his still crisp shirt as he laughed with the bartender in a long wordless roll. "Here she is, Joe," he said when he spotted Amanda and pulled her into his embrace. "I want you to meet my daughter."

The bartender smiled like bartenders do and held out his hand. "Name's Steve. Nice to meet you."

"Thought it was Joe," Mr. Easton said with only a moment of confusion. "Anyway, darling, what can I get you? A glass of wine? A real drink?"

"No thanks, nothing, Dad. I thought maybe we could go home, it's quieter there, and talk about whatever it was you wanted to talk to me about."

He smiled. "Sure. That's a wonderful idea. Why not? Let's go home. Time to find your mother."

"I meant my home, Dad." She tried to look encouraging. "C'mon, I'll cook you dinner."

Mr. Easton laughed and turned to Steve. "From what I hear, that's not much incentive."

"C'mon, Dad. It'll be nice."

"Sure, honey. Whatever you want. What do I owe you, Joe?"

"You're all paid up." Steve took some of the bills off of the bar and handed the rest back to Amanda.

He sat up straight in the cab, almost straight. He needed to talk to her, important. He sat up straighter.

"So, you're a woman," he said as they inched down Second Avenue, "you tell me."

"Tell you what?"

"How to ask her to marry me."

"Who?"

"What do you mean, who? Your mother, of course."

"What about Joan? Are you getting a divorce?"

His eyes strayed out of the window, a woman had four tiny white dogs on four long leashes. "Joan. Went to see Joan."

"Like this?"

The woman disappeared around a corner and he came back inside and smiled. "No. This is what comes after, darling, after. But it's okay." Straighter, he sat up straighter. "It's better. Today, today was, but anyway, it's better, I promise, you'll tell your mother, won't you? that it's better, she'll listen to you."

"Did you tell her where you went this time?"

He didn't answer.

When they pulled up in front of her building, Amanda tried to pay the driver, but her father put his hand over hers and then rustled and rummaged through his wallet until he found a reasonable amount of money.

Sam looked up from his paper and watched their concerted attempt at a dignified entrance. He looked up and scoured his factory of smiles until he found an appropriate one. "Hi."

"Hi." Amanda borrowed one of his smiles. "My father's decided to come over for dinner."

"That's great. How are you, Mr. Easton?"

Mr. Easton laughed. "So formal. You're such a formal young man. Mr. Easton. So formal. Dad would sound ridiculous, I agree. But shall we settle for Edwin? Not quite Mr. Easton, not quite Ed," he was laughing still, amused by this formal son-in-law of his. "What do you say, Sam?"

Sam nodded uneasily. "Of course. Whatever you'd prefer."

"I'd prefer Edwin."

"Fine."

Satisfied, Mr. Easton nodded and walked into the living room and settled carefully down onto the couch while Sam followed Amanda into the kitchen.

"What do we have?" she asked, not looking at him. "What can we make?"

He watched her open the cabinets and the refrigerator and even the silverware drawer, he watched her, and it was only dinner, it was nothing, what can we make for dinner, what is there? Nothing?

"Let me do it," Sam said.

"Fine." She walked back into the living room and sat down on the couch beside her father.

"Nice place," he said.

"You've been here before."

"Not in years. You never invite me. Why don't you ever invite me over?"

"That's not true. I've invited you over. You're always off someplace."

He reached across her suddenly and picked up the phone, examined it for a minute, and then put it down. "Do you think she'll say yes?" he asked as his eyes slipped around Amanda's face until they finally settled on her mouth.

"She always does."

"What does that mean?"

"Nothing, Dad. Yes, I think she'll say yes."

"Yes, I think so too. But you never know. You just never know, do you? You'll tell her, won't you, that it's better now?"

Amanda could hear Sam filling up the pots with water for spaghetti and rummaging around for things to throw into a sauce, her father listened too.

"He's a good man, isn't he?"

"Yes."

"You take care of him."

"I will."

"People have to take care of each other."

"I know, Dad."

"Do you?"

"Yes."

"I hope so. Is he gentle?"

"Why do you ask that?"

He smiled and touched her hair, the way he used to, when she was his, that way. "Because you're so impatient," he said softly, "you need someone gentle."

She wasn't hurt or hard to it, not now, not anymore, she only nodded and said, "He is."

Mr. Easton looked at her for a moment and then he stood up and began to search for his coat.

"Where are you going, Dad?"

"I think it's time I went home."

"I thought you were staying for dinner? Stay for dinner."

He smiled tenderly as he picked his coat from the chair. "You've already done your job."

Amanda could only follow as her father passed the kitchen and stuck his head in. "Good-bye, Sam."

Sam looked up from his stirring, surprised. "Good-bye, Ed."

She closed the door behind him. She locked it and she slid the chain into place and she walked down the hallway and into the bedroom. When Sam found her, she was lying on her back, thinking nothing, nothing at all. He lay beside her and she rested her head on his shoulder while he touched her cheek, her hair, anywhere he thought it might help.

"Is there anything I can do?" he asked.

"Just hold me."

He nodded.

"I hate him for doing this to you," he said, as he rubbed her back in circles. "He has no right."

She let his hands go round and round, circles, nothing, round and round. "It has nothing to do with rights," she said finally.

He continued to hold her, to massage her. "Yes it does. Why can't he just leave you out of it? Lay his mess on someone else's door, not yours. He shouldn't do it to you."

They lay quietly for a few minutes, round and round, nothing, and far away they could hear the water boiling over onto the stove.

Her lips folded into her gums and then out. "Look," she said, the circles, the round and round, beginning to irritate her skin instead of soothe it, "I brought a ton of work home that I have to get done by tomorrow." And she slid out of his embrace and walked back to the corner she had dropped her portfolio in and then she spread it out on the living room floor, spread out the sketches, the figures and the placements and the xeroxes of contracts, it was nothing, only this, this row of paper, all lined up, all diagrammed, this and nothing more, she began to shift some photographs to the left and to the right, her head bent close, and she hardly noticed when Sam walked by her into the kitchen to throw away the dinner that had surely hardened into long leaden strips.

She sat at the table and watched as Sally cleaned and then cleaned what she had just cleaned.

"Anyway," Amanda went on, "I guess he's back home. As far as he's concerned the whole thing never happened."

"Maybe he doesn't remember. That's nothing new."

"Oh, he remembers. He wasn't that drunk. Almost, but not quite. That's the funny part. I think he called me so that he wouldn't get that far. Some sort of half-assed new strategy of his."

Sally had a lotion-soaked Q-tip in her hand, going into the tiny crevices of the stereo cabinet, behind the dials, under the arm, it was a good thing to do, as good as any, better.

"I don't know what good he thought I could do though," Amanda went on. "What do you think?"

"How should I know?" Sally snapped. "You're the one he called, not me." She dropped the Q-tip into an ashtray and wetted a new one. "What did Mom say?"

"I don't know. Nothing. The usual."

"What do you mean, you don't know? You just told me you talked to her this morning."

"She said he was there. That's all she said. What does she ever say? I don't know if he asked her to marry him or not. Frankly, I don't see what the big suspense is. I mean, can you imagine her refusing? It's all she's ever cared about."

Sally blew onto the stereo needle and turned around.

"I know." She wiped her hands on her stained jeans, front and back. "You know, they say it's inherited."

"What is?"

"Alcoholism."

"I know, but we've talked about this before. I don't think either of us are alcoholics. Do you?"

"No. But," she paused, flicked away a few strands that had freed themselves from her ponytail, "but I do think there's something, I don't know, maybe we have a missing gene, something spliced, or unspliced, I don't know, something."

Amanda crossed her legs, to run and to run, something. "What do you mean?" she asked warily.

Sally turned suddenly businesslike, straight up and sure and starchy. "You see," she said, "I think we both have a tendency, though I have to admit it took you a little longer to find it, to look to others for stability. And then, when we find it, we feel a need to rebel against it." She had a debater's briny eyes.

Amanda groaned. "Where did you get that one from? A radio call-in show?"

"I started seeing a new doctor in January. I'm going without Frank this time. Maybe you should consider it."

"There's nothing wrong with me."

"Well, she's really helping me to understand a lot of interesting things."

"And all in just one month."

Sally frowned. "It has to do with having an alcoholic father. You and I may have reacted differently, and maybe we lucked out of the odds, though I'm not always so sure, but anyway, there's something off, and it comes from the same cause. Trust me. It's common," she went on, the words, the intonations, someone else's, someone she believed, but someone else's, not her words, not her intonations, not yet, "for children of alcoholics to have an irrational fear of being found out. Think about it."

"I'd rather not."

Sally raised her eyebrows. "See?"

"Christ, Sally, you asked me to come over here and tell you what happened. But I don't remember signing on for family therapy."

"You're making a big mistake. I can't tell you how much better I feel since I've begun to face up to certain things."

"So are you madly in love with your husband, are you having sex ten times a week, have you flushed your secret stack of Valiums down the toilet, have you finally decided to join the work force and take over IBM?"

Sally's mouth retreated, held itself still for a moment, Amanda's did too. But suddenly, Sally laughed. "I said I'm making progress. I didn't say I believed in miracles. So tell me, how did Sam handle the Dean Martin routine?"

"Fine. He was fine. He's very supportive."

"Not like Frank, is that what you're saying?"

"I didn't say anything about Frank."

"You didn't have to. Never mind. Now what?"

"What do you mean, now what?"

"What do we do now?"

"About our husbands?"

"About our parents. I mean, there's really no point in talking to either of them," Sally said. "Nothing we say is going to change them."

"That's a switch for you."

"Well that's what the shrink is teaching me. You can't change other people's behavior, you can only change your own. So what's the proper etiquette here? Do we throw them an engagement party with white ribbons and bows? How about a bridal shower for Mom? I can just imagine Dad's idea of a bachelor party, a five-day binge. What do you think? Should we treat them to a honeymoon at Betty Ford?"

"She hasn't said yes yet."

"Give me a break. Just give me a fucking break."

"I'm just so tired," she said. Her head was nestled by his and a loose strand of hair fell across his mouth but he didn't bother to push it away. "I know."

"Everything. Everything just seems to take so much energy lately. Everything is some kind of negotiation, the store, my family, Sam. Even Sam. Even we're always negotiating," she couldn't remember when she had started crying, "when we should go to sleep, what we should do about dinner, how much we should have sex, everything, everything, it's all some oblique negotiation, all of it. I just want to rest."

"Why don't you take a vacation?" Bill asked.

"How can I? The line debuts next month, Nancy only works part time, Sam can't . . . "

"Okay, I get the picture. Are things, I mean I know they seem testy now, but aside from that, are they okay between you two?"

"Sure. They're fine. I mean, there's nothing wrong."

His hand tightened about her waist. "Then why did you come here instead of going home?"

The Dinah Washington record had ended and it was quieter than before it had started.

"He didn't get it," she said softly.

"Didn't get what?"

"My father. He was sweet and protective and he acted like he was outraged and he tried to say whatever he could that might help. But he just didn't get it."

"You always told me that you didn't get it either."

"I don't. Only sometimes I do."

"What is it that you get?"

"I get that sometimes it all just stops, completely stops making sense, sense seems to dissolve, like you suddenly forget how to walk. Either that or it makes too much sense, it's suddenly so fucking clear that it just pierces and goes on doing it, piercing and piercing you with its sense. And that's when I think he drinks. That's what I think he's trying to escape when he disappears."

"But he comes back. He always comes back."

"He comes back. I know. He comes back. Yin yang in hell."

"Or at least the Upper East Side." Bill smiled gently. "It's chemistry, you know."

"So I keep hearing. But that's not what I'm talking about, Bill, you know that. It's about the place you can go, or try to go, where no one can touch you, that's what I think it's about with him. And you don't want anyone to touch you there and then you resent them for not being able to touch you there and love never seems to have anything to do with it. Maybe it does. I don't know. I know that he loves my mother, and me and Sally. And I know that you're probably right about the chemistry part of it too. But I still think it's more about that place where you can go when you don't even want to remember how to walk, when walking makes no sense, somewhere far away from that, just for a little while, before it all finds you again, before all the hands come back on you again. Just for a little while, you know?"

"Well, it certainly sounds like you do." But then he put his arm around lower, tighter. "Yes. I know."

She resettled her head on his shoulder. "Why can't Sam touch me there, Bill? Why not?"

"I can't answer that." He rearranged his legs slowly, carefully. "Do I touch you there?" he asked.

"No. Yes. Sometimes. I don't know. At least you know what I'm talking about."

"How do you know Sam's not feeling the same way? How do you know he's not wondering why you're not inside of each other too?"

"I don't know that, I don't know that at all. That's what makes it so hard. I don't even know if what I'm missing exists, if it ever exists, except in those false flare-ups at midnight, I don't know if he feels it too, if he misses it too. Maybe he doesn't, maybe he doesn't want to, maybe it's what scares him the most. Or maybe it's all in my mind, maybe this really is it."

"And maybe you don't want him to reach you there, maybe it's what you're most scared of too. Maybe you haven't even given him the chance."

She smiled. "A game of maybes. Maybe if I tried, tried to, Christ, I don't even know what, whatever it is, show him, get to that place, maybe he would run and run and never stop running away from it, from me." She patted his leg and a little tidbit of laughter came out. "He likes neat things, you know."

"You just told me you don't know what he feels."

"I don't know what you feel either, not really. But at least I don't always feel like I'm struggling for vocabulary with you. It's funny, but I think part of the problem with Sam and me is that I'm always just trying to find a way to describe it to him, the mystery, the place, whatever, and he's always trying to find a way to codify it, to solve it, you know? Sometimes I think he just shakes his head at some of my ideas."

Bill smiled. "It's always hardest when it's the biggest risk, when there's something to gain, something to lose. It's easy with us because we're not taking any risk. We gambled it away a long time ago."

She left them there, on the top of his desk, she left them out.

Amanda picked the extra blanket off of the bed and tried to fold it into a neat series of rectangles but the corners obstinately refused to meet. Cursing it, she crumpled it up into a ball and dragged it like a brat to the linen closet where she threw it in the back and slammed the door behind it. She would not think about it.

She stormed into the bathroom and washed her face, splashing it again and again with water that was far too hot—she would not think about it—and then buried her face in a towel that did not smell quite fresh. She lost herself in the mirror for a moment, her face ragged, wan, lost herself in the lines about her mouth that were still recent enough to be questioned anew each morning—are they visitors, or are they here to stay?—she tried to lose herself. She shook her head sharply. No, she must not think about it. She reached resolutely for a bottle of foundation and began to spread it in quick circles into her skin. But when she tried to line her eyes with a charcoal pencil, her hands began to quiver . . .

It was all she could think about, all she could see, the neat black lines of handwriting, all about him, all about her, atomic shadows, the pages and pages of it, the woman in the blue shoes and the man, and more, more, what did he call it, the walls, the miles and miles of walls, in him, in her, the neat black handwriting that fell between them like a dam, the bricks and the battles and longing in his heart to wipe it all away, the scrawls where the pen had run out and he had switched to another, her dancing and her death fears and her lost hours in the dark, that too, the neat black handwriting, etched like a curse into her chest . . .

She was in the living room now, picking up the container of juice that lay sideways on the table and crumpling it in her hands, the last pulpy drops falling silently to the floor. She crouched to wipe them up and she stayed there . . . an incoming tide of lunacy, he had written, an incoming tide of lunacy—she didn't know if he meant the city or if he meant her, she didn't know he felt it too—the neat black lines that he hid behind, the saddest of boundaries, the saddest of keys, to maps she hadn't seen, an atlas of fear where nothing ever felt real . . .

When the front door opened, she stood quickly up, fighting through a rush of dizziness to glare at him, at his walls and his alcoves and his atlases, at his neat black lines like an indelible curse, she glared at him, the stranger.

Sam walked in, smiling as usual. "Hi."

"Hi." She cut the word in half and the blunt edge banged into him as he stood in the closet hanging up his coat.

"You okay?" he asked.

"Wonderful." The neat black lines, all in a row, pulsing away like an organ in a dish, a liver, a heart, a spleen.

He stepped out of the closet. "What's the matter?"

She grabbed the notebook and flung it at his feet. "This."

He stared down at it, at the red marbleized cover lying on the gray wood floor. And then her.

"You went through my desk? You went through my fucking desk? Through my notebook?"

"That's not the point."

"What the hell do you mean, that's not the point?

What other point is there? How dare you? The one thing, the one thing in the whole damn world that's mine, that's just mine."

"I'm not sorry. I'm not one bit sorry. You stole all of it, all of us, you hid it all, all of you. How was I supposed to know? I never would have known, not about any of it. I'm not one bit sorry, goddamnit."

"Never would have known what?"

"Any of it. The walls. How nothing feels real. Any of it. Why didn't you ever tell me? I feel like I've been living with a stand-in, a fucking mannequin."

"I don't believe it. You went through my papers and you're the one who's mad at me? You're fucking unbelievable, Amanda. Do me a favor, save your outrage for another day."

He bent over and grabbed the notebook and headed to the closet, to his coat, to the door.

"Wait, Sam."

He was going and going, he was going away from her.

"Please. I didn't mean it. I am sorry. I was wrong. I just didn't know what else to do, how else to find out, please . . ."

But he had already slammed the door in her face.

He walked.
The red notebook on the gray floor.

He walked and he walked and this time he didn't see anyone, not the people in front of him, not those pushing past him, this time he did not hear footsteps behind or in front of him, this time, he was following nothing, he just walked. The red notebook on the gray floor. He walked and he held it in his hands, tightly, though it was no longer his, not now, not anymore. He kept walking.

He walked and walked through streets that were nothing but tarnished silver, nothing but gone, she had stolen it, the red notebook on the gray floor, stolen the only place he had left to go. He walked. Across to the West Side where the wind flew off of the Hudson River and cleaned the streets of strollers and up past the hooks of red cow carcasses hung in naked rows, now taken in for the night so that only the stains of their blood remained, the red notebook on the gray floor, out and stolen and gone.

He walked, back east, through curving brownstone streets lined with pitiless barren trees, and he tried to open it as he walked, but the neat black lines only blurred before his eyes, he shut the covers and tried to remember what was in it, what he had committed.

Slowly he felt the chill air climb into his coat sleeves and his jeans. He walked east four more blocks and stepped down into his café, into his alcove, to see if that at least was still his.

There were only two or three people left and he chose a table in the back corner, he wanted walls around him, and waited for the waitress to pull herself reluctantly from her chair to take his order. "Just coffee?"

It was the bottom of the pot and the bitterness and the grounds stuck to his tongue. He placed the notebook on the empty chair opposite him and after a couple of more sips he took off his coat and carefully folded it and placed it over the notebook. There was no place left to look but out.

There was only one man left at the other end of the café, a sad balding young man whose eyes flitted over Sam and then back, down into his cappuccino. He rested his head heavily in the palm of his hands and his lowered lids formed pink half moons. Sam looked away, down into his own coffee, anyplace, trying to remember what it was like to be inside, to be warm, to be safe.

The red notebook on the gray floor.

He stirred the grounds in eddies and licked them off of his spoon.

He wondered if she had found what she was looking for.

He looked up and watched as the balding sad young man was joined by a friend and his sadness seemed to sink inside where you could only see it with a flashlight as they left the café together.

He was the only one left.

The waitress walked slowly over to the deserted table and picked up the single cup with one hand and wiped the black top with the other, her eyes turned sideways to Sam as she straightened up and carried the cup to the counter. The blues tape ended and no one put on another one, not another one, she started piling the chairs legs-up on the table tops.

"I guess I'll take a check," Sam said across the room to her.

She nodded and ripped the top sheet off of her small green pad and walked it over to his table.

Sam dug out his money and put it on the table and he picked up his coat and his notebook. The streets were matte with night cold, but he walked slowly. There was no place left to go but home.

In the morning, she was waiting for him. He had come back last night but he was still out and out and gone and so was she. But now she was waiting for him. He attempted to smile but it didn't work and she didn't smile back and his mouth slid down into a rest bit. She would wait quietly, she had been waiting for as long as she could remember, she could wait now.

Sam stepped carefully out of the tub and tried to appear easy, tried to pull the skin closed over what she had opened, as he lathered his face and began to shave, each motion, each flick, as fragile as the first time he had stolen his father's razor and tried to erase a nonexistent beard.

She watched, waited.

One stroke, the next, again, breathe evenly, concentrate, regulate, again.

The corner of the razor bit into his cheek and he flinched, wondering whose hand had caused it, hers or his, but he said nothing as he reached across her and ripped off a piece of toilet paper.

Still, she watched, waited.

He dabbed the cut and little bits of yellow tissue grew crimson and soggy and stuck in minuscule fragments to his soapy face.

She watched, waited.

He threw the tissue in the waste basket.

"I've been wondering," she said at last, "if you bled

like other people, or if your blood just formed perfect little ice cubes.''

She stood up and walked out of the room before he could applaud her performance. He finished shaving.

When Sam walked into the bedroom to dress, he found Amanda seated on the bed, half-naked, crying not in sobs, but in a slow stream as thick as tree trunks.

''Why didn't you tell me?'' she asked.

''Tell you what? That I wrote? You knew that.''

''No. Not really, no. I didn't know anything.'' Her voice was quivering under water. ''Is that what I am to you, an incoming tide of lunacy? Is that what you're always guarding against? Is it?''

He sat down on the bed beside her. ''Not you. Not just you.'' His voice was deeper than it had ever been. ''But yes, sometimes, all of it, the city, our lives, all of it, yes, sometimes that's what it feels like.''

''And the walls you wrote about? You think they'll keep it all out? Or do you want to keep it all in? Away from me, safe. Is all you want to be safe?''

They couldn't look each other in the eyes.

''All I know is that you have to at least try to control it,'' he said.

''Why?''

''Because I don't want to live a life of chaos, that's why.''

''Either, or. It doesn't have to be either, or.'' When she turned to him there was ire shining through her tears. ''Did it ever occur to you that that's what I'm scared of too? Maybe a different kind of chaos, an inside kind, but did you ever think . . .''

''How could it occur to me?'' he answered harshly. ''Maybe you didn't write it all down and put it in a drawer, but you keep it all just as hidden.'' He kicked at the rug with his bare toe. ''An inside kind of chaos? Is that what you think you're going to outrun? All you really do is end up chasing it instead. Christ, I can't even believe we're having this discussion. You had no right, Amanda, none."

"It's too late for that now."

They both got lost inside themselves for a moment.

"You know sometimes," Amanda said, "sometimes I think you're happiest just sitting back and longing for what you think is on the other side, an armchair traveler. Okay, maybe not happy. But that's what you do, you sit there on top of your walls and well, it's no wonder you trace strangers in the street. It's no wonder nothing ever feels real. You don't let it."

He flinched.

"Sam, don't you know you'll never find it, whatever it is, whatever you want, never get past those walls, never even stand a chance, unless you're willing to pay your money and jump?"

He stared at her. "Jump? Sometimes I think all you ever do is jump, jump, jump. Why are you so damned scared of standing still? What are you so scared you're going to find?"

She was quiet for a minute. "I don't know. The same. An incoming tide of lunacy." She smiled briefly at his words that fit so perfectly into her mouth. "Scared of running in place, isn't that what you called it? Scared of stopping. Scared that I'd always feel lost. Scared of being like everyone else, dead. Scared of not finding you."

They let it stay there for a moment.

"You betrayed me," he said. "I still think you betrayed me."

"We betrayed each other." The tears weren't running out, but changing, changing into fat slow-motion drips. "Sam, you want to hear something really funny?"

"What?"

"You remember all that better and worse, sickness and health stuff?"

"Yes?"

Her smile was sad and ironic as a widow's. "I believed it."

He lowered his eyes.

"Really," she went on, "once I finally decided to do it, I believed it more than anything else, more than heaven and hell, more than anything. I mean, it made sense to me. It just made sense to me." Her nose was running and she sniffed loudly. "I thought we'd be partners, on the same side, I thought we'd be in it together. And now it just seems like an endless funhouse maze, the kind with all the crazy mirrors. All these other images keep appearing. I can't seem to remember what we looked like, it's so distorted, I can't seem to remember what we meant. Maybe we never even knew."

He bit his lip, removed the first layer of skin.

"But you want to hear the really pathetic part?"

"What?"

"I still believe it."

He reached over and ran his forefinger down the long blue vein in her neck, bit through the second layer of skin. "I know. I know. I do too," he said quietly, "I really do."

"I love you," she said, "even if . . ."

"Even if . . ."

They were simply stating facts now, no more, no less, they were comparing hands, this is what they had, it was something.

They were both watching, waiting.

"It's very complicated," he said, "isn't it?"

"Yes."

They were looking at it together now, as if it lay sprawled at their feet, picking up an arm, a leg, letting it fall—dead? alive? yes?

They were watching and they were waiting and they couldn't, couldn't watch anymore, couldn't see anymore, too many funhouse mirrors, couldn't find it there, couldn't wait anymore, and they moved slowly, rapidly, they moved desperately into each other, clutching each other's hair and backs, as they fell onto the floor.

"Harder," she moaned.

"Yes."

Harder, slamming against each other, violently, harder, until they could crash through it, find it, harder, seeking what lovers must once seek: annihilation.

Spent, they had landed, where? upside down, half on the floor, half off, they had no idea how, it was very complicated, they lay tangled up in each other, and she leaned over and instead of kissing him, she licked his wound where the blood had dried onto his face in hard crimson flakes.

His pain was real to her. No one's pain, not her father's, not her mother's, not Sally's, had ever been this real to her, had cut like her own, as his did now. She supposed that this meant that she could, after all, love. She used to wonder.

It was not, then, a seventeen-year-old howling at the moon, it was simply this—looking across the table at someone and having his pain be real, cut like your own, more, doubled.

The Thai restaurant was dark, woody. In the fireplace, a fake log glowed an iridescent orange and aging poinsettias shed their bloody leaves across the balcony. The waiter brought their main courses, and they began to eat. They each took mouthfuls of chicken satay, put down the wooden sticks, drank. Sam was describing an island he had just read about off the coast of North Carolina, remote, unspoiled, wild. Perhaps there?

"Sam," she said, interrupting his description of the local vegetation, "what are you going to do about it?" An incoming tide of lunacy, in him, in her, in the neat black lines.

"About what?"

"The notebook."

"What do you mean, what am I going to do?"

"I saw the stories too."

He poked at the peanut sauce with his skewer.

"And they were good. Why didn't you ever tell me about them?"

"I didn't think they were important."

"Oh c'mon."

"They were in the past."

"But you wrote how much you missed working on them. How much you resent what you're doing now. I was pissed as hell that you kept so much hidden from me, but . . ."

"I didn't know you'd go through my desk."

"Whatever. Anyway, the point is, I don't think following strangers in the street is going to give you the answer, but I do think even the way you wrote about that, the way you described them . . ."

"What makes you think there is an answer?"

"There has to be something."

"Something. You have these ridiculous immediate responses. Quit. Do this. Don't do that. Christ. What if I did decide to quit *Backlog*, start again, go back to the stories or real reporting, whatever. Has it ever occurred to you that I might be giving up my best shot?"

"Shot at what? Security? That's a precious price to pay, don't you think? Besides, you can't really believe that *Backlog* is your best shot. I refuse to believe that."

"And sometimes I can't believe how little you think about the future. What would happen if I did what you wanted, tried to, and then I woke up and found myself suddenly middle-aged, empty-handed, found out that I was just kidding myself after all? What then?"

"I'd rather have that than wake up at sixty and find out that I'd never even tried, that I'd been so scared of the slightest bit of uncertainty that I . . . besides, Sam, why not assume that it will work, whatever it is you decide you want to do?"

"You make it sound so simple."

"I know it's not simple. But I also remember when we first met, when you would talk about reporting, I had so much respect for the way you . . ."

"Had? Does that mean you don't respect me now?"

"Maybe it means that I have more respect for you than you do."

"What does that mean?"

"It means that you should just follow your heart and stop looking left and right and left and right all the time, stop weighing all the damn odds and just do it, whatever it is that will make you happy, and the rest of it will fall into place, all the lunacy and the uncertainties and the walls."

"You're suddenly awfully sure of yourself, of all this."

"No I'm not."

"No?"

"No." She smiled that fleeting half-smile. "But it sounds good, doesn't it?"

The waiter walked slowly by to see if they were finished and then he walked away.

"I do think, though," she said, "that there has to be middle ground."

"And where's your middle ground in your late-night ramblings and all your knocking on wood, huh? Where's your middle ground when you're running in circles so fast that you can't even see the ground you're standing on?"

"I didn't say I'd found it." She took a sip of her wine, put it down, looked at him. "But that's what I thought, that's what I always thought the real point, the point of us, was, that maybe, just maybe, we could find it together. Sam, I know that I don't have the answers, I know that I have just as many walls and just as many convoluted fears of lunacy, just as many ways of hiding as you do, I know that, but I'm willing to try, to try slowing down, willing to stop and look at it, whatever it is, for the first time, I mean, I'll really try to stand still. But you have to meet me halfway."

He looked at her. "What about money?"

"Why does it always come down to money with you?" she asked, exasperated.

"Maybe because I never had any. I never took it for

granted. It's real easy for you to sit there and tell me to quit, to give me this wonderful follow-your-heart line, but that doesn't feed anyone."

"Yes it does."

"I'm not talking about your metaphysical bullshit. I'm talking about the rent."

"I told you before, I'll pay the rent for a while. That's just about the least important thing I can think of right now. You can get a part-time job if you want, at night or something, but just take some time out, figure out what you want to do, a different kind of reporting, real reporting, features, your stories, I don't care, just find it and follow it and don't let it go."

He sat completely still. "Why are you so sure of all this?"

"I'm not. I only know it's worth the chance."

"Oh yeah?"

She smiled. "Yeah."

The waiter passed by again and this time he took their half-empty plates away from them. There were people waiting at the door.

"Who knows," Amanda said, "miracles happen, right? Maybe one day we'll even trust each other."

Sam laughed. "I didn't know I married such a dreamer. What happened to the hard-bitten, fast-walking, cynical city girl?"

"You never really fell for that, did you?"

"I fell for a lot of things. I'm still falling."

Amanda smiled. "You know, they say the first year of marriage is the hardest."

Sam smiled too and looked down at his watch. "How much longer do we have left?"

"Y"ou're wrong." Nancy pointed once more to the third necklace on the table. "You're absolutely wrong. Look again. If you photograph this one, all of the detail will get lost. It's got to be the earrings."

"Maybe if we just went ahead and got the guy who specializes in this it wouldn't get lost."

"I thought we'd agreed he was too expensive. You told me we could use, what's her name, Lucy."

"I can't stand her. She annoys me. Besides, this card is important. It's the first thing the press is going to see."

"Why are you telling me all this now? I thought that we had settled it yesterday."

"You settled it. I didn't settle it."

"Yes you did."

"Not really."

"You mean you're being honest now and you weren't before?"

"Okay," Amanda said, "yes."

"Great. Why didn't you just tell me how strongly you felt from day one?"

"I should have. But I didn't. Anyway, I am now."

"Now that we have three days to get these cards done."

"Look Nancy, I've done a pretty good job so far. Will you please just trust me?"

"You've been pretty scattered lately."

"What's that supposed to mean?"

"I mean that the party is in two weeks and the pieces are just now ready and the cards haven't even gone out."

"Let me just do it my way, okay? I can handle it."

"Christ," Nancy said, straightening up, "do whatever you want. Just get them out."

"Fine." Amanda walked briskly over to the phone and dialed the number she had in her hand while Nancy went out front to check on Deirdre. After a brief conversation, she grabbed the necklace and her coat and walked quickly out.

"He said if I ran over to his studio right away, he'd photograph it now," she explained on her way to the door.

"Well you know, I wasn't planning on staying in the store all day today."

"Nancy."

"Okay, okay. Just come back as soon as you can."

She stood in the corner and tried to keep her hands from moving it this way—the curl right at the nape, does he see it? he must, but does he, will it show, I have to be able to handle this—she stood in the corner and watched in the dark, it only took a few minutes, could he have done it that quickly? he couldn't have done it that quickly, how about one more roll? No, you're sure? Well, if you're absolutely sure, of course I trust you, it's just . . . Yes, thank you, yes, I appreciate you fitting us in, really I do, yes I have it, thank you . . .

When Amanda walked back into Legacies an hour later, Nancy was in the back going over the guest list one last time.

"How did it go?" she asked, looking up.

"Fine." She didn't quite look at her. "He seemed to know exactly what to do. He promised it would look terrific."

"That's great."

Amanda hung up her jacket and began to unwrap the necklace and put it back with the rest of the work.

"Listen," Nancy said hesitantly, "I talked to Jack a few minutes ago."

"Oh?" Amanda turned partially around.

"Yeah. Anyway, I gave him a good dose of feminist guilt and he said he'd go home early tonight and stay with the baby. So what do you think?"

"What do I think about what?"

Nancy smiled. "Girls' night out."

"You're asking me out on a date?"

"Since when were you so hard to get?"

Amanda squinted her eyes. "Where?"

"Where? Anywhere. I don't care. A movie, a club, dinner, dancing. Anyplace I'm guaranteed not to get saliva dribbled in my ear."

"Well that rules out most of New York."

"How about it?"

"I thought you had become a resolute homebody?"

"Everyone's allowed a night of escape every now and then. Maybe I'll even remember to leave the baby wipes behind. Though it's been so long since I've been out that for all I know they could be a new sex tool."

Amanda laughed.

"Besides," Nancy added. "I think, I just think it would be good for us. Don't you?"

"Absolutely."

Nancy smiled and nodded and then she went back to her list. Amanda watched her bent head for just a minute before she went up front to help Deirdre unpack a box of antique hats.

It was just like any other morning. Sam sat at his desk editing the copy on the latest crop of young British menswear designers, he sat at his desk just like every other morning—except that he had been working on the same page for almost an hour, the type fading in and out of his vision like a half-forgotten dream. He took a sip of the coffee that had grown cold in his lost in out interims, put it down, changed a single apostrophe, stared at it, and then suddenly he stood up. His legs moved until he found himself inside the glass partition of Patrick's office.

"Do you have a minute?" he asked.

"Sure, come in. What is it, the layout?"

"It's time for me to leave," Sam said abruptly and he listened to the words as if someone else were speaking.

"What? You mean you need to take the afternoon off? You're past having to ask permission, you know that."

"No. I mean I have to leave, move on."

Patrick leaned forward onto his elbows. "You're not going back to Ohio again, are you?"

"No, it's not that."

"Do you have another job? Who for? Tell me."

"It's nothing like that, Patrick."

Patrick leaned back, took a slow survey up and down. "Money? Is it money? I'm sure we can work something out."

"It's not money," Sam answered, it was easy as a

free fall. "It's just time for me to move on. Do something else. This was never what I had in mind."

"Look, Sam, I know that I promised you more features, but you know how tight pages have been. We've been going through some growing pains, you know that. But it's going to even out and you'll be able to have a little more freedom, maybe even your own column again. Just be patient, okay?"

"It's not good. It just doesn't make any sense." Easy.

"What's not good? What doesn't make any sense?"

"We'd both be kidding ourselves, Patrick."

"Tell me, tell me what it is you want."

"I don't know. Not exactly. More features, of course, more . . . I don't know. I just know that it's time for me to move on." He dug his hands into his pockets. "I'll stay, of course, until you get someone to take my place."

Patrick twirled his hair around his gold pen. "Of course. Well it shouldn't take long. The city's crawling with talented editors looking for work. People call us all the time. I just thought you were here, though, for the long haul."

"Well, I'm glad it won't be too difficult for you."

"I appreciate that."

"And I'll finish all of the pieces I've been working on."

Patrick nodded. His phone was blinking by his hand and he took one last curious look at Sam before he nodded imperceptibly and picked it up. Sam watched him and waited for a moment, could it really be so easy?, and then he turned around and walked back to his desk, back to the latest crop of young British designers.

He picked up his pencil and stared once again at the copy, it was all raw and giddy, it was someone else's, not his, it was someone else, not him, all raw and giddy and laughable, yes, that too, laughable, why not? gravity was miles away. He shook his head and focused his eyes down, the cut of pants legs would certainly be looser, baggier next season, and his pencil began to veer through the lines with quick and steady motions.

All afternoon, he edited page upon page, he made up a list of story ideas, he congratulated three different writers on their style, it was far away now, far enough for him to enjoy it, yes, why not? it wasn't him after all.

And when he left the office that night, he walked quickly, he almost ran, through the streets that once again seemed swollen, untried, giddy and raw and new, through this shiny swollen city to tell her.

Sally had announced over a week ago her intention of having a special family dinner to celebrate the recently announced engagement of the Eastons.

"Are you out of your mind?" Amanda asked skeptically. "I thought you were against the whole thing."

"Whatever the state of my mind may or may not be, I think it is the proper thing to do," Sally said firmly. "Even Frank agrees."

Now she stood in the dining room and fixed the centerpiece amid the carefully ordered barrage of china and individual butter dishes, miniature salt and pepper shakers and heavy silver serving spoons. As she gave the lilies in the center a final touch, Maggie watched with huge up eyes, careful in her new velvet dress.

In the kitchen, Frank basted a turkey, his face flushed from the oven's heat. Satisfied with its progress, he shut the glass door, and then peered out at his wife. He watched her closely, carefully, he watched for warnings, as she stood fussing even now with the table that had been set and reset for hours. Only the ringing doorbell kept her from turning the plates so that the gold rims would be in even more perfect accord.

It was all quite lovely, really. Sally leaned back in her chair and surveyed the table, the family, her eyes narrowed as if to gain a better, or at least different, perspective. They were all behaving so well—they really were such a perfect imitation. She watched Frank at the other end, meticulously slicing a piece of white meat on Maggie's plate. He caught her glance and looked up, smiling briefly, hopefully, and then he smoothed his daughter's hair, waiting for her to look away. If only conversation wasn't such an obvious strain, they could almost pull it off. She took a sip of her wine, put it down, returned to her periscope, to this perfect puppet family that only needed a script. That's what she had forgotten, how stupid of her. She let out a short laugh that caught everyone's attention, and she looked quickly at Maggie as if she had done something humorous. She would have to be more careful.

"Well," Mr. Easton proclaimed, putting his arm around Mrs. Easton's chair, "we've finally come to a decision. Hawaii it is. Just where we went the first time round." He turned to Amanda and Sam. "What about you two? Weren't you going to go on a honeymoon? I don't understand why you'd want to leave out the best part."

"We will," Amanda answered. "But right now we're trying to save some money."

Sam fidgeted beneath the table. "I told you we could go," he said.

"No, I'd rather wait." She turned to her family. "We'll go when Sam sells his first piece."

"Right," Sam said.

"Well, I think it's lovely dear. Just what kind of writing is it you're going to do?"

"I'm not exactly sure yet. I'll probably start trying to do some free-lance pieces. Features. I know a few people."

They all chewed, swallowed, took another mouthful, chewed.

"He's a natural born reporter," Amanda said.

Sam frowned. "So," he said, turning to Frank, "how's the public relations business going?"

"We've gotten some big new accounts recently," Frank answered, and he began to describe them, the intricacies and the challenges of representing a baby food manufacturer, a foreign car maker who specialized in faulty brakes, the Marines. Sam nodded and asked leading questions while Mr. Easton drank his soda and thought about Hawaii and Mrs. Easton thought about the husband she had won back and Amanda thought about bracelets.

Suddenly, in the middle of Frank's description of how to hide the sugar content of baby goop, Sally stood up and whispered, "Excuse me." They all pretended not to watch as she made her way hurriedly from the table to the master bedroom.

". . . sweet as baby himself," Frank continued, "you've got to put it something like that. You see?"

Sam nodded. "Aren't there certain legalities involved?"

"Of course, but . . ."

When Sally had been gone for over five minutes, Amanda, who had decided to alternate bracelets with necklaces in the front display case, decided to go check on her.

She walked down the hallway, past years of framed vacation photos—Sally and Frank on the steps of the Coliseum, Sally, pregnant, on a Spanish beach, Sally holding Maggie in front of a weathered barn—and knocked on the closed bedroom door. "It's me," she said quietly, and walked in, finding Sally sitting up on the bed, her high heels digging into the white goose down quilt. She clutched a pillow tightly to her chest.

"You okay?" Amanda asked, sitting down beside her.

"Of course I'm okay." Her eyes were wide, unfocused.

"Dinner was wonderful."

"Was it?"

"Yes."

"Oh."

"Sally," Amanda played with the scalloped edge of the pillow sham her sister held so tightly, "I've been thinking about some of the things you said that day."

"Forget all that."

"No. I think, well, I don't agree with all of it, but some of it made sense. Maybe we both have to be more careful."

"I've been careful for so many years I've forgotten how to be anything else."

"Did something happen since then? You seemed so sure of yourself. Are you still going to the same doctor?"

Sally shifted her head but her eyes stayed still. "She thinks I should leave him."

"I didn't think doctors were supposed to tell you things like that."

"She didn't just come out and say it. But I just know it's what she thinks."

"Well, you've talked about it before."

"I know. It's just so . . ." her voice wandered off to wherever her eyes were.

"Well, whatever you decide," Amanda's hand moved from the pillow to her sister's knee, "I'm on your side."

Sally tilted her head and smiled. "I don't seem to know what side that is anymore."

Amanda smiled too. "Whatever."

They sat for a few more minutes in the quiet bedroom.

"Well," Sally said, straightening her hair, "should we go back out into the ring?"

Frank had already set up dessert and the seven of them began to eat their crème caramel in silence.

"No one has made a toast," Sally said finally. "Why hasn't anyone even offered a toast? Well I will if no one else will." She raised her coffee cup and the others followed, holding the delicate china in midair, waiting. "I'm not sure who to congratulate in this instance," Sally said. "Let's see. What do they say in these instances? Well, there never really are quite these instances, are there? May you always be as happy as you are tonight. Is that good? May you . . ."

"That's fine, honey," Frank said and he took a sip of his decaffeinated coffee and everyone else did too.

It had begun to flurry when Sam and Amanda finally left with her parents, finding them a cab first, and then searching for one of their own.

As they looked out of the window at the weightless pricks of white, Sam turned to Amanda. "Your sister," he said, "was high as a kite."

Amanda flipped the top of the metal ashtray, let it snap shut, flipped the top of the metal ashtray, let it snap shut. "She'll be okay," she said at last. "She'll be fine."

Enormous posters of steel bracelets, copper necklaces and intricate earrings circled the room like a party of amputated extremities. The slanted Legacies logo shone from the lightboard overhead and the room sputtered and coughed with the sixteen artists who had contributed work, the galleries who represented them, reporters and photographers from the *Times, Vogue, Backlog.* Amanda stood inside a cluster of friends and acquaintances and strangers, still glossy with a nervous excitement that was just beginning to wane. Copper earrings dripped down almost to her collarbone and already her lobes ached—she would have to talk to Neil about that. Across the room, she spotted Nancy and Deirdre in clusters of their own, both adorned in an inordinate amount of jewelry.

"So toots," Bill said, pulling her aside, "you did it."

Amanda glanced about the room and then looked at Bill. "You think?"

He smiled. "I think. And I really am impressed." He leaned over and kissed her. "How are you? Better?"

"Better? Yes, better. Much better. How about you?"

"Me? I'm always the same. Copacetic is my middle name."

"That's not true," Amanda said gently. "But it's okay."

He smiled. "It's okay."

She leaned over and returned his kiss. "Do me a favor?"

"Is it illegal?"

"Not yet. Will you just go over and talk to Sally? She

263

came by herself tonight, some sort of trial balloon, I don't know, anyway, she was doing fine, but she seems to be temporarily stranded. Just go keep her company for a few minutes, okay?''

Bill smiled. "Sure."

Amanda watched him as he went over to the bar and got two glasses of champagne and brought one over to her sister.

At the other end of the restaurant, Sam stood talking to Patrick as Lucy scampered at their feet, snapping pictures of the walls, the women, the *Backlog* staff, the long-haired man in the blue bow tie. He watched her shapely scuttle, he watched the banal pronouncements slide out of Patrick's mouth, he watched Mrs. Yatnikoff, who had lately become something of a *Backlog* mascot, fight for the camera's eye, he watched, amused, as the details no longer got in the way—they were no longer his. When he walked away from them, they hardly even noticed.

Her back was to him, bared by an embroidered dress from the early thirties and he ran his finger down her spine before he pressed his torso up against hers and the surprise and the familiarity and the endless otherness of it shivered through her. "I'm proud of you," Sam whispered in Amanda's ear.

She turned around, smiling. "The *Times* said they loved it. They might even do a feature next week. With photos."

"That's great." He rubbed a tiny speck of coral lipstick from her front tooth with his thumb. "Can you leave yet?"

"I don't know," she said hesitantly.

"You've been here for hours. Surely you've talked to everyone you have to."

"I know. But can't we stay out, just tonight?"

He smiled at her. "Of course. But I just thought we could go someplace special. By ourselves."

She swam into it, the smile and the blue of his eyes and the boy of him. "Where?"

"Anywhere."

She smiled too and kissed him. "Okay, look, let me just say good-bye to Nancy. And Sally. And . . ."

Sam laughed. "Okay, okay, forget it."

"No really, it'll just take a minute." Her head twisted a little to the left. "I want to be with you too."

"Okay. I'll wait outside."

Amanda went over to where Bill and Sally were standing side by side in the corner. "I just came to say good night," she said. "Thanks for coming."

Bill laughed.

"Okay, but you know what I mean."

"Sally and I were just going to have a late supper," he said. "Why don't you and Sam join us?"

Amanda smiled. "Not tonight." She leaned over and kissed both of them good-bye and headed off in search of Nancy.

Sam stood out on the street, a few feet beyond the black velvet ropes and the doormen. The harsh edges of winter were beginning to wear away and he left his coat unbuttoned as he watched Deirdre slip out of a side door with her latest beau. When Amanda finally came out he put his arm around her and kissed her fully on the lips before they started walking. The streets were a shimmering night map of blackness and colored lights.

"So tell me," Sam said as they crossed Fifth Avenue, "now that you're this huge success. Will you still love me if I'm painting other people's apartments three months from now?"

"I'll still love you."

"Will you still love me if I'm reduced to writing pornography under an alias?"

"I'll still love you." She smiled. "Especially if it's good."

"How about if I hit fifty and still haven't figured out what the hell I want to do?"

Amanda laughed and wiggled her hand, maybe, maybe not. "I'll still love you," she said. "I might not like you very much, but I'll still love you."

Sam smiled. "It must be some sort of character defect," he said.

"Must be," Amanda agreed and they stopped to kiss.